Call of the Whales

'An adventure with attitude'
THE IRISH TIMES

'A captivating coming-of-age tale with a
distinctive narrative voice'
THE IRISH INDEPENDENT

'Parkinson's reputation as one of Ireland's most talented
storytellers for the young can only be enhanced by this
powerful, yet wistful work, which will illuminate the
imaginative lives of its readers, no matter what the age.'
BOOKS IRELAND

SIOBHÁN PARKINSON

Siobhán lives in Dublin with her woodturner husband Roger Bennett, and her schoolgoing son Matthew. She is writer-in-residence with Dublin Corporation and the Irish Writers' Centre (1999–2000).

Her previous books include *Amelia, No Peace for Amelia, All Shining in the Spring* and *The Leprechaun Who Wished He Wasn't*. Three of her books have been recent Bisto award winners: *Sisters ... no way!* won the Bisto Book of the Year; *Four Kids, Three Cats, Two Cows, One Witch (maybe)* won a Bisto Merit Award, and *The Moon King* won a Bisto Merit Award also. *Breaking the Wishbone* is her novel for young adults.

Call of the Whales

Siobhán Parkinson

THE O'BRIEN PRESS
DUBLIN

First published 2000 by The O'Brien Press Ltd.,
20 Victoria Road, Dublin 6, Ireland.
Tel. +353 1 4923333; Fax. +353 1 4922777
E-mail books@obrien.ie
Website www.obrien.ie
Reprinted 2001

ISBN: 0-86278-691-6

British Library Cataloguing-in-Publication Data
A catalogue reference for this title
is available from the British Library.

2 3 4 5 6 7 8 9 10
01 02 03 04 05 06 07

The O'Brien Press receives assistance from

the arts
council
an chomhairle
ealaíon
50⊦

Editing, typesetting, layout and design: The O'Brien Press Ltd.
Colour separations: C&A Print Services Ltd.
Printing: Cox & Wyman Ltd.

GLOSSARY

Eskimo: A controversial, collective term for many arctic peoples, including Inuit and Inupiat. Many people, particularly in Canada, find the word 'Eskimo' offensive, since it is not a word in their language and has been imposed by outsiders, mainly white people. However, 'Inuit' cannot always be used as an alternative, because not all the peoples who are sometimes thought of as 'Eskimos' are in fact Inuit. This makes it a bit difficult to talk about these peoples in general, without using the term 'Eskimo'. In Alaska, to add to the confusion, some people use the term 'Eskimo' to refer to themselves. I've tried to avoid 'Eskimo' for the most part and to use the correct term for each group in this book, and hope readers will not find it too confusing.

Inuit: Term, meaning 'human beings', used to cover many different groups of arctic peoples, mainly those living in Canada, parts of Alaska and Greenland (although the Greenland Inuit usually refer to themselves as Greenlanders or Kalaallit); the singular is Inuk.

Inupiat: An Alaskan people who live partly by whale-hunting; the singular is Inupiaq. It means 'human beings'.

Kalaallit: The Greenlandic word for Inuit.

Kayak: Light one- or two-person skin-covered boat.

Maktak: Whale skin.

Mukluks: Snow shoes.

Nalukataq: Major festival held at the end of the spring whaling season to celebrate the success of the whaling.

Pod: A family group of whales. A pod can be as few as two or three whales, or as many as thirty or forty, depending on the type of whale, the season and where they are.

Taig: A variant spelling of the Irish name, Tadhg, meaning 'poet'. Throughout the book Taig is known by his nickname, Tyke.

Umiaq: Light wood-framed boat, covered in walrus skin or seal skin, large enough to take a whole whaling crew and the whaling equipment but light enough to carry over the ice on a sled.

AUTHOR'S NOTE

I have taken liberties with my research material, transposing stories and names and words from one part of the Arctic to another, for the sake of the fiction, but I have tried to be as accurate as I can without overloading the novel with detail. I hope I have managed to respect the spirit of the Arctic and that Arctic experts will forgive a certain amount of fictional licence.

I believe that it is the right of peoples of all cultures to tell their own stories in their own way. This doesn't mean that outsiders may not sometimes, with respect, tell other people's stories too, but it is of course much trickier to do that well. For this reason, I have deliberately told this story of Arctic life from the point of view of an Irish narrator. And that is all this novel is meant to be: an outsider's perspective on a rich and fascinating way of life in a place of great beauty.

I would like to acknowledge a detailed account of present-day Inupiat whaling by the Danish television journalist Adrian Redmond; several documents by the anthropologist Norman Chance; some fabulous photographs and a most interesting account of his time spent at Thule airbase in the far north of Greenland by Larry Rodrigues; and some terrific material on the official Greenland government tourism Internet site, www.greenland-guide.gl.

The story of Sedna is retold here from a version I read on the site www.cancom.net/~sedna (accessible through about.com). The polar bear story is adapted from one of Norman Chance's articles.

I am grateful for the support of the Irish Writers' Centre and Dublin Corporation Arts Office, where I held a joint residency during the time this book was being written, and of An Chomhairle Ealaíon/The Arts Council who part-funded the residency.

Because books should where possible
be dedicated to those who love them,
this one's for you, Liz.

CONTENTS

Prologue

The song of the whale is like a call to the north. I hear it in my sleep. Eerie and sonorous, it pervades my dreams, so that I am drawn down into the deep, where huge sea beasts roll slowly in the inky-cold seas, wailing for their lovers over acres of waters.

I wake, gasping for air, from these whaley dreams, but even though I wake, I cannot seem to shake off the dream. All day the whales are with me, as I work my way through my city schedule – breakfast, train, work, lunch, work, drink, train, dinner, TV, bed – swishing their powerful tails, diving uproariously to the seabed, drifting in the depths and then slowly, slowly, like the air leaking out of a tyre, ballooning up and up and up to crash onto the surface once again and exhale their fabulous fountainy breath.

They are with me always, the whales, and yet they aren't, not the way they were when I was a child. But what can you do? You grow up, things change, you settle into your own particular you-shaped groove in the great economic machine that is modern life. You do your best to live up to the ideals you had as a youngster, but you can't linger for ever in that blue-lit, dreamy childhood world of the arctic north. It's not practicable. It doesn't pay the rent. And it's not your world. It belongs to other peoples. If there are rents to be eked out of that icy waste, it is for those people to do it, those tough and hardy, broad-faced, wide-eyed, dark-haired people whose bloodlines go back and back and back into the lost and snowy worlds of the arctic past.

It was meeting Henry last month that started it all. Geneva is not my favourite city, I have to say, but it's where a lot of these international conferences get held, because it is neutral territory. I'd slipped out of a plenary session to get a cup of tea. They don't make proper tea on the Continent, so I try to stick to the coffee. But there comes a point when you just have to have tea, even if it's lukewarm, served without milk and has a stout little teabag in it, anchored to the cup-handle by a string and a paper tag.

There was no one else in the canteen – they were all still at the meeting – so I was able to explain to the Swiss attendant how I wanted my tea made. '*Boil* the water,' I pleaded. He looked at me as if I was mad, but I added, 'I'm Irish,' and he nodded, as if that explained everything – which it did.

Then I heard the laugh, coming from somewhere behind me. My body did a little on-the-spot leap, as it does when I am startled. I spun around. I'd thought there was no one else in the canteen, but I could see now that there was a large black leather sofa with high sides facing the window. Slumped in one corner of the sofa, so that he was almost hidden from view, was a man dressed entirely in black and with hair so black it matched his black T-shirt and his black jacket and the black leather of the sofa.

'Irish!' he spluttered, shaking his head. 'The Irish and their tea!'

What do you know about the Irish? I wanted to ask, noticing his wide, dark-eyed, delicately boned, oriental-looking face, scrunched up now with laughter. He looked like people I'd known years ago, people I'd met in the Arctic. I could see he was enjoying the joke so much – what joke? I thought – that I couldn't bring myself to snap at him. I just smiled and waved vaguely and went to sit down at a table where I wouldn't have to look at this laughing man in black.

I'd just settled in my chair, resolutely facing the wall, with my back to the window, when I felt a tap on my shoulder. Not my friend again, surely. It wasn't like an Inuk or an Inupiaq to interrupt a person who clearly wanted to be left alone. They are a polite and silent people. But then I heard my name, or rather my old nickname, a name I hadn't heard for years, not since I was a boy.

'Tyke?'

My real name, Taig, is not easy to pronounce unless you're Irish. They'd always called me Tyke in the Arctic, and I'd got to like it. I had a campaign going for a while to get my family to use it, but they never really got the hang of it. It was strange to hear it now, all these years later, in this place.

I turned. At first I didn't recognise him. I thought he was someone else, another childhood friend. It had been almost twenty years since I'd seen him, after all. People change a lot in twenty years, especially if they were only eleven or twelve when you knew them before.

'Henry!'

Recognition came in a flood and I leapt to my feet. We stood staring at each other, delighted, but not sure how to act, too embarrassed to hug. Eventually, I slapped him on the upper arm, and he slapped me on the shoulder.

It turned out we were both attending the same international conference on whaling. I was there as an environmental activist, to make sure the big commercial whaling nations didn't get away with their plans to strip the oceans of as many sea-mammals as they could kill. Henry was there to plead the case of subsistence whaling, the lifeline of the small arctic communities, environmentally sustainable and essential to the culture of his people. To outsiders, it might look as if we were on different sides of this debate (he pro-whaling and I anti-whaling), but actually we were on the same side against the big boys with their huge killing ships and their money-driven lust for death.

It was wonderful to meet Henry again after all these years. We'd lost touch since we'd known each other as boys. I'd lost touch with everyone from those days, with some of the best friends I ever had – though it is only now that I realise it.

Henry had been to Ireland on a visit, he told me. He'd gone there, half-hoping to find me, but he didn't know my surname, so he couldn't look me up. We didn't want that to happen again, so we exchanged phone numbers and email addresses.

Henry works as a journalist now, in Anchorage, covering Inupiat affairs. It was hard to believe that the spindly, jokey boy I'd known all those years ago was now a respected writer and opinion-maker. I'm sure he found it just as difficult to believe that I am a college lecturer. I teach history, and I have long vacations that allow me sometimes to pursue my other main interest – protecting the world's whales.

We rejoined the conference after I'd finished my tea, and we met again for a beer that evening. Next day the conference was over, and with renewed promises to keep in touch, we both flew out of Geneva.

It's since meeting Henry again that the dreams have started. I've never lost the interest in whales I acquired as a boy, but it was only when I met Henry that I felt again the excitement I'd known in my youth when I used to visit the wide arctic wastes. It was Henry who reminded me of why it was that I took the interest that I did and it was meeting Henry that stirred up the memories which now invade my sleep and arouse in me an unrealisable longing for child-hood adventure.

The Unicorn Horn

I grew up knowing for sure that unicorns existed. You've probably seen pictures of these fabulous creatures: white, horse-shaped, prancing, lowering their fine heads to show off their splendid barley-sugar-twisted horns, with their silken manes flowing in the breeze that is fanned up by their own swift flight. People have told you that unicorns were magical horses that lived in the once-upon-a-time. When you asked where you could find one, they'd say unicorns were extinct now, or that they'd only ever been imaginary beasts, like gryphons and dragons, and the only place to see one was in the coat of arms of the queen of England.

But I knew they were for real, and the way I knew was that we had a unicorn's horn at home. My dad brought it back from one of his expeditions years back, before I was born. It was a magnificent giant spiralling ivory object, about five feet long – much longer than I was for most of my childhood. I have no idea how my dad got it home from the northern beach where he found it. He'd have had to lug it back to Dublin, via Copenhagen or Reykjavik or Moscow and Heathrow. It wouldn't have fitted in the overhead lockers in the aeroplane, and I couldn't imagine that he would have packed it like a pair of skis and put it in the hold with the rest of the luggage, because it was hollow and quite fragile. If he tried to bring an object like that through customs today, he'd be arrested for importing ivory. But when I asked him how he'd managed it, he never answered. He just tapped the side of his nose with the side of his index finger and winked.

He said this was quite a small unicorn horn – that he'd seen specimens up to nine feet long. I couldn't begin to imagine how big a horse would have to be to have a horn that long.

The other thing about unicorns I knew that other children didn't know was that they were sea creatures. I knew this because my father said the horn we had at home had come from a beach and was all that was left of a sea unicorn. That made sense to me, because after all, the horses you read about in all the great stories – the fabulous white horse that Niamh and Oisín rode to Tír na nÓg, for example – were able to ride over the seas, and there was every chance that they were really sea unicorns.

To tell the truth, the horn in our sitting room looked a bit yellowish, like a gigantic, gnarled and twisted old tooth in a way. But I imagined it as the unicorn must have worn it, all bright and pearly white in its youth, gleaming blue-white like a baby-tooth, and maybe – I knew this was a bit of a cheat, really, that I was making this bit up – maybe the spiralling shape was traced with just a thin line of gold, like a seam of gold leaf running along the twisting length of the splendid horn.

When I was very young, and my father was obliged to stay home from his travels in order to look after me, we would look at the unicorn horn, and my dad would tell me that one day we would travel together to the land where the unicorns ruled the waters. It was many, many years before I discovered what those words really meant. In the meantime, I allowed my imagination to run wild, conjuring up that land of sea unicorns my father visited, and of course I saw myself riding these magnificent creatures, and I was always wearing a long blue velvet cloak lined with stars of gold.

Arctic Summers

I suppose I was only about eight or nine when my father first started taking me with him on his expeditions. We always seemed to arrive in a rickety little old propeller-powered plane, skimming in across the treeline – the point beyond which the winds are so harsh that no tree dares to grow unless it's a dwarfed juniper or birch or willow that slinks sneakily across the rocks, hugging the ground. Over the scrubby tundra landscape we'd glide, coming in to land somewhere north of civilisation. From the plane you could see the whole hummocky flatness of the countryside spread out and rumpled like a badly made bed, the hillocky tundra plains ablaze in sudden masses of blue-spiked lupin, wild crocus, mountain avens, arctic poppy and saxifrage, and dotted with lakes and rivers. Occasional gigantic lumps of ice would still be hunched here and there, quietly dissolving in the long, lingering summer sun. The villages were huddled, higgledy-piggledy assortments of wooden houses, just dropped any old place, it seemed, facing all directions, with no discernible streets.

It all looked unkempt and makeshift and not the sort of place a boy like me would want to spend his summer holidays. Not a swimming pool in sight or a cinema, not even a playground or a nice clear surface for roller-blading. But hey, I was going camping with my dad and we were up above the Arctic Circle and *anything* could happen!

My father was an anthropologist. That's 'a posh word for nosy', my mother used to say. (My mother was English. They talk like that, the English.) When I was a kid, I thought 'anthropology' had something to do with 'apology', because my father was always apologising for intruding into people's lives. (He wasn't nosy at all by nature, or not in the way my mother meant.) As soon as our plane landed, he'd put me sitting on the rucksacks beside the runway and he'd go and find somebody to apologise to. Depending on how well the apology went down, we could stay or we might have to move on to the next place.

Nowadays, most arctic people live in houses like the rest of us, and have central heating and spaghetti hoops and hospitals and Coca-Cola vending machines, but in those days there were still places where the people lived a more traditional way of life. Naturally enough, the local people were often a bit suspicious of an Irishman landing among them with a tape recorder and a notebook, but my dad always said I brought him luck when I went with him. When people saw that he had a kid along, they thought he must be OK. They took their kids places with them and taught them stuff, and they thought of it as the right thing to do, so having me with him certainly helped – pardon the pun – to break the ice for my dad. The people usually said it was all right for us to set up camp and live in their villages and for my dad to do his work of observing and listening and writing about the way they lived, even if they thought it a bit odd.

So we'd set up our tent in the lee of an old wall or an aeroplane hangar – any sheltered place we could find. Then we'd heat up some baked beans on a camping stove – it always seemed to be baked beans on that first night, easy to carry, I suppose – and pump up our air-mattresses, and after we'd eaten and washed up, we'd snuggle up in our tent and lie awake, watching the shadows created by movements outside rippling over the nylon tent roof.

For the people whose winter is an endless night, the endless days of summer have to be lived to dropping point. Even the children played way past midnight in those few weeks of high summer when the sun never left the sky.

I'd lie there behind the thin tent walls listening to the children's voices laughing behind rocks or whooping from the roofs of huts and outbuildings. I couldn't sleep while they played, and they played, it seemed to me, endlessly. When exhaustion finally overcame them at one or two or even three o'clock in the morning, their older brothers or uncles or dads or cousins came and carried them heavily home to sleep in rooms darkened by drawn curtains, while outside the birds still sang and the poor confused owls hunted in broad daylight.

It was a strange, upside-down sort of a life for a lad from Drumcondra. And even after the children had finally gone home to bed, I would still lie for ages listening to life being noisily, brightly lived just feet away from our tent in the small hours of the morning, and the strangeness of it all stirred up a small earthquake of excitement in my stomach.

Looking back, all those trips we took, all that moose jerky and fish we ate, all those freezing places we landed, all those endless summer days – a lot of it has merged into one undifferentiated memory. My father's research took him all over the Arctic – to Alaska, to the Yukon in Canada, to Labrador, to Greenland, to Siberia, anywhere that there lived peoples of the Eskimo races. Once you're in the north, and especially the further north you go, you lose the sense of which country you're in anyway. The Arctic is its own country in a way and has its own weathers and customs and practices.

But as I say, it all blurs a bit for me now, and I couldn't tell you an Inuk from an Inupiaq to save my life, though maybe the differences were clear at the time. Nor can I speak a word of those amazing languages my father used to practise late at night in our tent, reading by the light of the midnight sun from a heavy hard-backed book and testing out sounds in Yup´ik or Inupiaq. But I do remember particular incidents and people, and the friendships forged in wild northern places still glow for me like bright beads of experience in the murky shadows of my childhood past.

Meeting Turaq

I don't remember their names, those boys and girls I found dabbling in mud-patches behind hut-houses or lying on their stomachs on icy banks and watching seals following their noses up the food-rich channels between the breaking ice, except that they had strange, sharp names for a strange, sharp part of the world. But I do remember Turaq.

'Where you from?' he asked, the first time we met.

I think it was Canada, the Yukon, though I really couldn't be sure. I couldn't tell you the year, either, though I imagine I was about ten or eleven. But the details I remember with great clarity.

He didn't say hello. He had broken away from a group of younger children who were playing some sort of game I didn't understand.

'Ireland,' I said, pointing in a direction I imagined to be south. It sounded to me as if this boy didn't speak much English, so I spoke carefully and used the minimum number of words to explain myself. 'Long way away. Europe.'

'Ah.' He nodded and smiled, and then he went back to join his friends.

He was shorter than me, but Inuit are shorter anyway, and I reckoned he was about my age or maybe a bit older. He didn't play much, but he seemed to be in charge of about three smaller children. He spent a lot of his time picking them up and swinging them in the air and helping them to catch up with bigger children in the games.

The local children played oddly, it seemed to me. I'd never really seen kids play together in that way before. Where I came from, kids played *against* each other. Play was a sort of continuing battle, everyone wanting to win, everyone wanting to be king of the castle. Those were the rules I understood. I didn't know how to play their way, and I watched and watched, trying to get the hang of it, but I never did really work out how the rules of Inuit games went.

After a bit, Turaq came over to me again. I thought maybe he was going to ask me to join the game, but that didn't seem to occur to him. He said nothing for a time, just stood beside me and watched the younger children. Then he asked: 'You fish?'

Well, I'd fished in the Royal Canal, and I'd even fished once or twice for mackerel on Dún Laoghaire pier, but I knew that wasn't what Turaq was talking about. Around here, fishing was a serious business. It wasn't something you did on a Saturday afternoon between lunch and the match. It had to do with food. So I shook my head.

'Tomorrow,' Turaq said, 'you come fishing?'

I shook my head again. I didn't have the equipment, for a start.

'You come,' he said, and he went off and gathered up his three young charges.

4

Turaq to the Rescue

My dad said of course I should go – it would be a great experience, he said – just so long as I promised to let Turaq take charge. I had no intention of doing anything else. I knew who the expert was around here.

So the next morning I went to the place behind the schoolhouse where I'd seen the children playing, only half expecting to find him. We hadn't made a proper arrangement. Nobody'd mentioned time, for example. But there he was, hunkering over his fishing equipment. He smiled at me when he saw me, and he handed me two large fishing nets. He carried a big wooden contraption that was designed for a traditional method of trapping fish.

'Turaq,' he said to me.

I shrugged my shoulders, thinking he was saying something in his own language.

'My name,' he said carefully. 'It's Turaq.'

It was quite a big deal for someone like Turaq to give his name away like that to a complete stranger, though I didn't understand that at the time. I concentrated on trying to pronounce my own name as clearly as I could, but he didn't quite get it.

'Tyke?' he tried.

That was pretty close. For a foreigner. Goodness knows what sort of fist I would make of Turaq.

I repeated my name.

'Tyke,' he said again.

That would do. I liked it. I smiled, and we set off for the spot at the mouth of the stream where Turaq wanted to set up his trap. We were fishing for arctic char, though I didn't know that at the time. Turaq told me the local name of the fish, but I couldn't even pronounce it then, never mind try to remember it twenty years later. It was my dad who told me they were char, and they tasted wonderful, like trout only much, much more so. They swam in the freshwater lakes and they crowded down the fast-flowing meltwater summer streams and spilled joyously out into the frigid waters of the sea, and it wasn't long before we had trapped several of them. Turaq showed me how to use the net to lift them out of the trap and how to tap them on the head to stun and kill them, so that they didn't thrash about and leap back into the water. We laid our catch into a light canvas bag that Turaq had brought along for the purpose. There were far too many fish for one family to eat, but Turaq told me his mother would freeze or dry most of them for winter food.

What happened next, I can't really explain. It wasn't that we were fooling around. We were just standing about, talking. At least, I was listening, and Turaq was talking in that funny, hesitant way of his. It wasn't that Turaq didn't speak much English, though that's what I thought at the

25

time. Even then, English was the language of the state and of school, and everyone except the old folk spoke it. It was that he didn't speak much at all. None of the Inuit people went in for long speeches. They communicated much of the time in some mysterious other way that I couldn't work out, no matter how hard I watched them at it.

Anyway, we'd finished fishing for the day, and I know I was standing on a rock with my back to the water. Nobody pushed me. It just seemed to happen all by itself. I suppose I must have lost my footing on the slippery rock, though I don't remember that part, but suddenly I felt myself jerk backwards, my arms outstretched and my legs flailing helplessly. It felt as if I had gone briefly into suspended animation: I could picture myself, like an upside-down spider, all limbs, and then my body just dropped. I knew I was falling, but I couldn't prevent it. Next thing I knew, I hit the water. It wasn't deep, but I had been standing right at the point where the racing, meltwater-swollen stream came seething down from the narrow riverbed and shot into the sea, and I was pushed several yards out into the freezing waves by the furious force of the stream.

I will never forget the iciness of that water. It was cold beyond cold, so cold that I experienced it not as cold at all but as pain. Down I sank into inky, salty, freezing pain. And then I blacked out.

When I came to, I was in an agony of cold. I was lying on the tiny scrap of beach where Turaq had been standing, tidying away his fishing gear, moments before. It must have been only moments, but it felt as if weeks had passed since I'd laid my last char, still thrashing weakly, into Turaq's canvas hold-all.

I opened my eyes and instantly closed them. My eyelids were amazingly heavy and felt caked with salt. When I managed to prise them painfully open, the sunlight stabbed the surface of my eyeballs. I could feel the earth shuddering with great thudding shakes, as if a huge goods train was chundering along just feet away. I knew there couldn't be, but I wondered briefly if there had been an earthquake. Perhaps that was what had tossed me off my rock.

Turaq's voice came to me, and I could feel his thin, stringy arms wound tightly around my torso, as if he was holding me down, like a mad person or someone having a seizure. Cautiously I opened my eyes again, and sure enough he had flung his body diagonally across mine and he was holding my arms tightly to my sides and we were both rattling away like nobody's business. Gradually, I realised that what was causing the rattling was me. My whole body was shuddering and trembling in a frantic effort to fight off the effects of the cold, and my teeth were chattering so hard, I kept biting my tongue and the pink, fleshy insides of my cheeks. Turaq was breathing warm, fish-flavoured air onto my face and down my neck and throat, into the top of my sopping shirt.

The rattling eventually subsided into a steady tremor, and Turaq rolled off me. He stood up and quickly pulled his sealskin parka up over his head and rammed it over mine. He didn't bother to try to jam my arms into the sleeves, just pulled it right down over my shoulders and tightened it in to my wet body. Then he yanked my head off the ground and pulled the furry hood around my ears. Warmth immediately settled around my aching head and shoulders, a seal-smelling, oily, fishy sort of warmth.

I became aware of the wet now, as well as the cold, and I wanted to tell Turaq to get my wet clothes off, but although I could make my mouth open, I couldn't get my jaw to work enough to allow me to speak.

Suddenly I didn't care about the pain, the cold, the wet. All I wanted to do was to let my poor numb limbs rest and to sink into sleep, but Turaq wouldn't give me peace to sleep. He flung his body onto mine again, and started that fishy breathing of his. I turned my nose away from him, and I could hear him give a soft laugh, but then I slipped off back into unconsciousness.

Next time I woke, I was still on the beach. Turaq lay beside me now, but still right up against my body, and though I felt miserably wet and cold, the dreadful numbing pain had eased and I was able to open my eyes and work my jaw.

'You wake, Tyke?' he said hoarsely.

I nodded.

'Uhh-kay. You stan' up now.'

Stand up! I couldn't stand up for a million pounds. I shook my head.

'You stan' up now, 'n' we go home.'

I shook my head again.

He pushed his hands under my back and started to lever me up. I resisted.

'You don' stan' up, you die,' he said matter-of-factly.

'I die,' I said, wearily. It came out as 'Aye-aye,' but Turaq understood.

'Uh-huh, not with me you don' die,' he said, and he levered some more, so that I was in a sitting position. Then he hauled me to my feet. I swayed. My body felt about as mobile as a sack of potatoes. I groaned as a wave of nausea washed through me.

Turaq grabbed me around the waist to prevent me falling over, and then he leant across my body and yanked one of my legs forward by grabbing a fistful of wet trouser-leg. Then the other one. And the first one again. And the other one. This way, he walked me back to the village like a giant wooden doll. Well, not quite all the way. After a while, I got the hang of this walking business, and I was able to move my legs myself, just so long as Turaq kept me upright.

5

Going Visiting

My dad said afterwards that Turaq had saved my life.

'I wouldn't have drowned,' I said indignantly. 'The water was only waist-high.'

'You can drown in a puddle if you're weak enough,' said my dad.

'I *wasn't* weak. Turaq *said* he didn't rescue me from the sea. I managed to pull myself out.'

'I know that,' Dad said, 'but he saved you from death by hypothermia.'

'Hyper-what?'

'Thermia, meaning heat, as in a Thermos flask. And it's hyp*o*, not hyp*er*. Hypothermia. What old people die of in winter.'

'I'm not old,' I said stubbornly, 'and it's summer.' I didn't like to be fussed about. I suppose I felt a bit stupid for falling in the water.

'Doesn't matter,' said Dad. 'It's summer, but this is the

Arctic. The sea is only just above freezing point, and anyone who falls into it can die within an hour unless someone warms them up, especially on a cool day like this.'

'Well, I wish he'd taken off my wet things first,' I said crossly. 'I felt like a squashed fish.'

'No,' said Dad, 'that's what you do – put warm dry clothes on top to trap the person's body heat, not let it escape by taking off their wet clothes.'

'Hmm,' I said. I knew he was right, that I'd been lucky that Turaq knew what to do, but he didn't need to keep going on about it. I was starting to squirm uncomfortably.

'And the other thing you do,' Dad said, looking up from his Arctic survival manual, where he had looked up 'hypothermia', 'is you get as close to the person as you can and let your body heat warm them up.'

'Body heat,' I said. 'So *that's* what he was doing. I thought he was being a bit ... cuddly.'

'Cuddly!' said Dad.

We both laughed then, at the idea of brave, silent, efficient Turaq acting cuddly. It was just all wrong. He probably wouldn't even let his mother hug him.

'Well, call it what you like,' said Dad, 'but it worked. You really could have died, you know.'

And he gave my shoulder a quick, affectionate squeeze.

'Dad?' I said, in a chokey sort of voice.

'Uh-hmm?'

'Mum doesn't need to hear about this.'

This was one of our man-stuff phrases. We said it to each other when we planned to keep our adventures to ourselves. Like the time I found Dad asleep on the sofa surrounded by empty beer cans. And the time I got three detentions in a week for … well, it doesn't really matter why, but it was not my proudest moment.

'That's right,' said Dad gravely. 'We wouldn't want to worry her, would we?'

Not worrying my mother was a great excuse for not telling her things. She had an artistic temperament, or so she said. This meant, as far as I could see, that she could get away with any sort of bad behaviour herself, but the rest of us had to behave impeccably, in case we brought on an attack of temperament.

She used to object to my dad taking me off on his expeditions with him. She wanted to keep me at home in our little terraced house in Dublin, but then she'd get offered work – she was an actress – and she'd be scooped off into that other, occasional world of hers, in a whirl of lunch dates and rehearsals and script-readings and voice sessions and studio days with the other 'talent' and she'd give up on the battle to keep me at home. I'd be better off with him, she'd suddenly agree, and did I have a snowsuit?

A snowsuit. She was thinking about the kind of thing small children wore to play in the Phoenix Park in the winter, to go sliding down the slides in, with bright mittens attached for their blue-cold little fingers. You see them all the time in cold weather on the toddlers. Primary colours and zip-fasteners. That was my mother's idea of what to wear in the Arctic.

Mum was the real reason I tagged along with Dad to these remote, icy places. She was a wonderful woman and we both adored her. She had a fantastic wardrobe, full of fabulous witches' shoes with high ankles and pointy toes and wondrous floaty garments in silver and black and champagne and she had the most marvellous bright red hair, but she was not what you might call reliable. In all conscience, my father used to say, you could not leave a child in her care for months on end. She was liable to forget she had me, he said, get up and walk out of the house and meet some friends and go off for a weekend to London and forget to come home to cook my dinner and send me to school. I don't know if that was really true – if it came to it, she would probably have shouldered the responsibility – but I suppose he couldn't take the risk. The safest thing, he always said, was to take me with him. That way I might be exposed to all sorts of dangers, but at least I would get fed and there would be a responsible adult around to look out for me most of the time. At least, that was Dad's theory. I'm not so sure about the responsible adult bit myself. Turaq was only ten or twelve.

Anyway, when Mum asked, of course I'd say I had a snowsuit. It would keep her happy, and having asked the question made her feel she was doing the proper mother-stuff. She didn't really know much about the mother-stuff, but every now and then she'd act like a mother. I mean *act*, not behave; act, like on stage.

I didn't really have a snowsuit. I wasn't three, and anyway, there wasn't usually much snow the places we went to in the summer time – at least, not in those early days. There was lots of snow on the horizon and pack ice to the north. But in the coastal settlements where we went to meet the people, the summer temperatures were mild to cool, but not cold, and the main problem was the mosquitoes.

The first time Dad showed me the tent we were going to take with us, I laughed when I saw that it had a built-in mosquito net. I thought mosquitoes were things you got in hot countries. How wrong can you be? We were eaten alive by the arctic mosquitoes, who were clearly thrilled to find some nice fresh Irish blood – a lovely change for them from the arctic blood they were used to. We were walking gourmet meals, me and my dad, in the arctic summers. It was the lakes that did it. The tundra is always pocked with lakes and boggy pools in the summer time. You could see that as you come zooming in by plane. It's because the ice melts and there's nowhere for all the water to go. Some of it finds its way into streams, but some of it just lodges in hollows and it can't seep away into the earth, because the subsoil is frozen solid all year round. So the water just sits there and creates a lovely damp environment for the mosquitoes to lay their eggs in.

Anyway, we agreed we wouldn't tell Mum, so as not to worry her. Dad didn't worry – or not so's you'd notice. He understood about risk – that's the good thing about Dad – and he knew I hadn't been foolish, just unlucky.

He said we had to go to Turaq's house, though, to thank him for saving me.

'*No*,' I said. 'I can't do that.'

'You have to,' Dad said. 'We are guests here, and we have to be very careful to be polite. Anyway, it's the right thing to do. He saved your life.'

'Don't keep *saying* that,' I muttered, embarrassed. But I combed my hair and brushed the twiggy bits out of my jacket and off we set that evening after dinner. I remembered to take Turaq's sealskin parka with me. We'd dried it out by hanging it inside-out over the tent ridge. I was glad I'd thought of it. It gave us an excuse to be going to his house. Saying thanks for saving my life was not my idea of a reason to visit someone.

I noticed Dad looking longingly at his tape recorder as we got ready to go, but I said, 'No way, Dad! You are *not* going to tape Turaq.'

'He might have a grandmother,' said Dad, wistfully.

'I'm sure he has,' I said, 'but she is Turaq's grandmother, not a "source" for you, not a "subject".'

I'd picked up a bit of anthropological jargon over the years. I knew that the way of life Dad was interested in was quickly fading and that the old people were the only ones who could tell him about the traditional way of life, but I drew the line at Turaq's family being used like that, for research purposes. He was my friend. It was different from just any family.

'You're right,' said Dad. 'It would be rude.'

'It certainly would be,' I said sniffily. I didn't often get a chance to tell an adult off. It's a nice feeling.

As it turned out, Turaq did have a grandmother. Turaq's father was away at the caribou hunt, but his mother invited us in. My dad was in heaven. His first invitation into an Inuit home that year.

I liked the inside of Turaq's house. Nothing matched. Even the two curtains on the living-room window were in different fabrics and of different lengths. It gave the house a lovely topsy-turvy, haphazard, colourful feeling that I liked, like being in a caravan. My mother thought she was dead unconventional, being an actress, but she liked her curtains to match and she was for ever 'picking up' the green in a picture with a scrap of matching green in the carpet or the little red stripe along the rug with a sofa-cushion in the exact same shade. It was what she liked to do, but I always thought it made our house feel stuffy.

Turaq's mother made us coffee, using a proper electric kettle – not very Inuit that, I could see Dad thinking – and offered us chewy meat to eat with it. I'd never had coffee with meat before; actually, I'd never had coffee. The combination tasted strange, but I suppose it was sort of … interesting. Dad said later it was jerky, which is a sort of dried meat. It was like gnawing leather, but tasty leather. Dad thought it might have been caribou or moose. The coffee was dreadful. I've always been more of a tea-man, myself.

Anyway, we said we had come to say thank you to Turaq. At least Dad did. I nearly died – again. Turaq smiled and bowed stiffly and his mother looked pleased. His grandmother smiled too.

Then Dad got all flowery. 'I don't know how we can ever thank you properly, Turaq. There is nothing we can do to repay you for your ki…'

I glared at him. You didn't talk to a ten-year-old about their kindness. That was too grown-up a concept. It sounded soppy to kids. I could never understand how adults could forget that sort of thing about being a child.

'For your … help,' Dad finished, glancing at me.

Turaq just nodded and smiled again.

Then his grandmother made a little speech. She leant forward and said to my dad: 'You don't need to repay Turaq. What you do is, when you see someone in trouble, you help them. That's how you repay a kindness. By helping the next person. And then they can help another person. And so it goes. That is the Inuit way.'

'A very wise old lady,' my dad said to me afterwards.

Load of philosophical old codswallop, I thought, but I didn't say it. I could see he was delighted with what Turaq's grandma had said. She was right, of course, though I didn't realise it at the time.

'That's the Inuit way,' Dad said to himself.

'Aren't you going to write it down in your notebook?' I teased him, snuggling into my deliciously warm sealskin parka. Turaq had refused to take it back. He said he had another one, and that I needed this one more than he did. I had reason to be glad of it, for many an arctic summer afterwards. I still have it somewhere, though of course it doesn't fit me now.

'Write what down?' Dad asked.

'What Turaq's grandma said. About the Inuit way.'

He laughed. And he didn't write it down. I couldn't work him out. But that's anthropologists for you. You never know what they're going to find interesting.

Shortly after that visit to Turaq's house we left and I never met him again. I never really got used to that – the way I would be just making a friend and then suddenly it would be the end of August and we'd have to go back to dreary, grey old Dublin and back to school and to other kids talking about their holidays in Courtown or Llandudno or trips to Old Trafford or stays in the Gaeltacht. It all seemed a bit … well, ordinary to me. But of course I couldn't say that. I'd say, 'Oh, Canada' or something very general like that when they asked me where I'd been.

'Ah yeah, Canada,' they'd say. 'Great. You're dead lucky. Rory has an uncle in Toronto.'

'Yeah, Toronto,' I'd say, secretly scratching my mosquito bites through the wool of my school jumper, and I'd nod as if I'd been there.

I never mentioned arctic char or midnight sun or hypothermia or names like Turaq. They'd think I was making it up.

6

Dreaming of Whales

My dad got a book about bowhead whales out of the library and we studied it together during that next winter. My mother had gone all dreamy and distant – I mean, even dreamier than usual. She took no notice of us and our books, just lay about a lot on sofas and ate cornflakes with hot milk.

They are magnificent creatures, those bowheads, forty, fifty, sometimes as much as sixty feet long, and forty to fifty or sixty tons in weight. Enormous is too small a word to describe them.

I couldn't get over the size of the whales. I kept looking at big things like a bus or a bungalow and saying to myself, 'A bowhead whale is bigger than that.' (And bowheads weren't even the biggest whales. There are much bigger ones.) It freaked me out that an animal could be bigger than a house. Not just taller than a house, like a giraffe, but actually bigger, much bigger. Bigger than *two* houses. Longer than a *garden*. (Longer than our garden anyway.) It was like trying to imagine a world full of *Tyrannosaurus Rex*, except that these creatures weren't prehistoric. There they were, in their hundreds, in their thousands, swimming their slow, undulating ways through the icy waters of the Bering Sea, swishing their enormously powerful tails, strong enough to make matchsticks of a boat. Right now, at this very minute, they were living and breathing and whooshing out their great V-shaped blows from their huge double blowholes, swimming and diving, lunging and plunging and waiting for spring. I couldn't get over it.

I kept trying to imagine what it must feel like to be a whale, how gigantic and lumbering. I wondered how long it would take to turn around in the water, for example – would you have to reverse a bit and then swing around, like an articulated truck? Or how long it would take for a message to get from your tail to your brain. And how much you would have to eat to sustain such a humungous body. It overwhelmed me, the thought of it all. It was like trying to think about infinity or how many miles away other galaxies are. My dad said that if you really were a whale, you wouldn't feel especially big. I thought that was daft, but he explained that from the point of view of an ant, say, *we* are enormous, but that we don't *feel* enormous to ourselves. I sort of saw what he meant, but I couldn't give up the idea that whales must know, must somehow have an inkling of how huge they are.

I read about how female whales made little families with their sisters and their young, and how the males joined them from time to time, but mostly hung about in gangs or lived solitary lives much of the year. I tried to imagine how they organised it all. I thought the females probably had a better deal, but then I tried to imagine a female whale giving birth in the freezing sea, bellowing with the effort of it, and with her sisters and her nieces all coming around to help and give her whaley support, and I almost drowned in the hugeness of it all. I imagined the calf emerging and I wondered how big it would be. Bigger than a cow? Bigger than a racehorse? As big as a camel?

The thing about sea creatures is, it's hard to believe they aren't freezing to death out there in the depths, isn't it? You try to imagine their lives, and all you can think of is the cold and the wet and the smell of seaweed and the taste of salt and the constant roll of the sea, and it all seems so difficult. It's very hard to believe that they wouldn't be more comfortable tucked up in a nice warm den somewhere, especially when you are thinking of mammals. Fish are different. You can accept fish, cold-blooded things, not minding the cold and the wet.

Dad got hold of a tape of whales 'singing'. They weren't bowheads. They were humpbacks. (The bowheads haven't made an album, it seems. They need a manager, my dad joked, but he said they made pretty much the same types of sounds.) We listened to the whales screaming like enormous, angry violins, accompanied by the steady splodging sounds of their tails thrashing the water, their voices gradually rising to a prolonged, agonising hooting sound. It made the little hairs stand up on the back of my neck. It was like a sick mermaid wailing in a cave, I thought, and the songs repeated and repeated and then repeated with a little variation, and then back came an answering song, from miles away, miles and miles away over the wide, wide ocean, like another distraught violin, lost and languishing and longing for its friends.

Meeting Matulik

As the sea ice starts to melt in the spring in the high Arctic, the whale book said, it cracks apart and open leads are formed here and there. This gives the bowheads, trapped all winter by the ice, their chance to pass, shouldering their way through the breaking ice, on their annual migrations to their summer feeding and breeding grounds in the Beaufort Sea.

'We'll go in the spring,' said my dad, 'when the bowheads start to move. To the northern coast of Alaska.'

'What about school?' I said. It was out before I'd thought it through. I probably should have said nothing.

'This is more important than school,' said Dad airily. 'You can miss a term. I'll help you to catch up later.'

Sometimes my dad could be magnificent. This was one of those moments. We didn't say anything to Mum about the whales. We just said we had to go early this year. She didn't say much. She didn't even argue that I shouldn't be missing school. She seemed unusually uninterested in us, come to think of it. She just asked her usual vague snowsuit questions, and we said not to worry, we were well equipped. She'd forgotten I had a fabulously warm sealskin parka, much better than any snowsuit available this side of the Arctic Circle.

Then she said, dreamily, 'Well, as long as you're back by September.'

I thought she meant for school.

We'd never been this far north before, and we'd never been in the Arctic at a time when there was still a little bit of night left over from the winter. I'd never seen the sun set up there before. It was like watching slow fireworks. Late, late in the evening, the high, bright, icy blue of the day seeped away into an apparently endless indigo twilight, and gradually the sky went pink and then pinker and pinker and it darkened to deep, deep orangey red, and then the colour faded and the light faded and everywhere was a sort of silver-lined navy, and that went on for a while, and that was the night, and then the sky pinkened up again and it was dawn.

Everywhere, the people were busy, busy. Every day the village helicopter flew out over the ice that stretched away across the sea, carrying some of the local men to inspect the ice, to see where the leads were breaking, because that was where the whales would be swimming. They hardly noticed us, there was so much to do.

Dad went straight to find a man called Matulik, as soon as we arrived. He was what they called a whaling captain in the village, and Dad had got his name from one of his colleagues as a good contact in Alaska.

'Hmm,' said Matulik, when Dad introduced himself, using the contact name he'd been given, by way of introduction.

'Yes, I heard you'd be coming. What you want?'

Dad fluffed and bumbled and muttered something non-committal.

'A teacher?' Matulik said.

'Yes,' said my dad. He lectured in anthropology, but he always used the word 'teacher' to explain himself, because people knew what that meant.

'What you teach?'

'I teach my students about the Eskimo way of life,' my dad said carefully. 'About your people's traditions and stories and ways of relating to the world.'

'Hmm,' said Matulik. He smoked thin yellow cigarettes and his fingers were as yellow as the cigarette paper. I envied him his pungent little cigarettes, because they kept the mosquitoes away. I was scratching already, even though we'd only been here half an hour.

'So you're an expert on our way of life, then?' Matulik continued.

'Oh no,' said Dad.

I knew he thought he was, so I was pretty surprised to hear him denying it.

'No, no,' he went on. 'Not an expert. *You* are an expert, Matulik. You and your people, you are the experts. I am just learning.'

'So what you want?' Matulik asked again.

'I want … my son and I,' said Dad, beaming at me, 'my son and I would like to come with you to the whaling camp.'

'Uh-huh,' said Matulik, and he took a deep drag on his cigarette. 'For why?'

'To learn,' said my dad.

I'd never heard him sound so humble.

'You environ-*ment*-alists?' asked Matulik suspiciously.

'No,' said Dad stoutly.

I had never heard that word before. I could sort of work out what it meant, but the way Matulik said it, it sounded like it was a disgraceful thing to be.

'You scientists?'

'No.'

'You oil people?'

Oil was a hot topic in those days in Alaska, with arguments raging between the US government and the native peoples about who owned the oil wells. They've sorted it all out now, more or less, and the local people managed to get a share of the wealth for themselves, but in those days it was a sore point. Oil was the last thing Dad wanted to be associated with.

'*No*,' he said emphatically, 'not oil people, not business people, not from the government. We don't belong to any organisation. We want nothing except to understand.'

'Hmm,' said Matulik. He still seemed a bit suspicious. He seemed like a man who had had bad experiences with strangers. 'But for why you want to understand? There must be a reason.'

'I'm interested in how peoples live,' Dad said. 'I'm interested in what makes societies work. I'm interested in what people tell their children, what they believe, how they explain the world to themselves, how they make sense of life … and death.'

'Life and death, huh?' said Matulik. 'I see.' But still he shook his head doubtfully.

He finished his cigarette and he stubbed it out carefully in an old cigarette box. Then he squashed the cigarette box in his small brown hand and pushed it into the depths of his pocket.

'OK,' he said. 'You want life and death, next week, when we got all the equipment ready, we break trail to the camp. You can come if you help. Him,' he pointed at me, 'he can be a boyer.'

'We'll help,' said Dad, beaming. 'Thank you, Matulik.'

'Where you living?' Matulik asked then.

We'd only just stepped off the plane.

'Well ...' said Dad.

'You talk to my wife. My son gone to Anchorage to work. You can have his room, that suit you?'

'Gee ...' said Dad, not letting on how ecstatic he was at the thought of actually living in an Inupiat house.

'OK,' said Matulik, and walked off with a vague wave.

'What's a boyer?' I asked.

'A boy who helps at the whaling camp,' said Dad. 'It's a great honour to be a boyer. It's a sort of apprenticeship for joining the whaling crew. You're very lucky.'

'How do you mean, "helps"?'

'Makes coffee. Gets snow to melt for water. Keeps the stove going. Watches out for polar bears.'

'Polar bears!'

'Uh-hmm,' said Dad.

'Dad! They're *dangerous*.'

'Oh, not usually,' said Dad, airily. 'They're like all bears. They don't bother you if you don't bother them.'

All I could think of was the big warning sign by the polar-bear enclosure at Dublin Zoo.

'Don't worry,' said Dad. 'There'll be lots of boyers. They'll know what to do. You'll have a fine time.'

Sometimes Dad could be magnificent. Sometimes he could be plain irresponsible. I wasn't sure which he was being just then.

8

The Man in City Shoes

The busyness continued for days. Everywhere you looked, people were packing things and checking things and getting things ready. There was a buzz about the place, and the children were in a state of high excitement. They were too excited even to stare much at me, which is what they usually did.

Then one morning a helicopter landed, right in front of Matulik's house. It wasn't the village helicopter. It was a government one, I think, or something official-looking anyway, green with brown markings – not very good camouflage colouring for this blue-and-white landscape.

A man wearing polished city shoes, a suit and a puffy anorak jumped out, his hair standing up like a shocked hedgehog in the whirl of the choppers.

'Matulik?' he bellowed, over the roar of the machine.

Matulik came out of the house, his hands clamped to his ears against the noise.

'Send it away!' he shouted, taking one hand off his head and gesturing wildly at the helicopter.

The city-dressed man gestured to the pilot, and the helicopter lifted and whippa-chunk, whippa-chunk, whippa-chunked away.

As soon as the noise dropped to a level where people could hear, the city man spoke to Matulik.

'The whale run this year has been unusually heavy,' he said, without greeting.

'Uh-huh?' said Matulik, his hands on his hips now.

'The next two villages down the coast have already caught more than their quota.'

'And?'

'Well, that means you can't go whaling this year. You people have already taken more than you're allowed. Don't you *talk* to each other? Can't you work it out between you?'

Matulik said nothing, just nodded and shook his head, nodded and shook in turn, his mouth twisted in an ungiving grimace.

'Well?' said the man.

'I got a telephone,' said Matulik in the end.

'*What*?' said the man.

'You coulda phoned me.'

'Oh,' said the man. 'I didn't have your number.'

'How many gallons of fuel you use to come tell me this?' asked Matulik, waving in the direction the helicopter had gone.

The man didn't reply. He slid his thinly shod foot along the ice underfoot and said nothing.

'You don' seem to me to be too concerned about the en*vir*onment,' said Matulik, 'if you can ride up here in a chopper to tell me a message you coulda telled me by phone.'

'I told you,' said the man. 'I didn't know you had a phone. I don't have your number.'

'Well, next time, why don' you check the phone book?' said Matulik, and turned back towards his house.

'Do I take it that you'll cancel the hunt from this village?' called the man.

'Take what you like,' said Matulik. 'And take yourself outta here pretty damn fast.'

He didn't look back. He walked right into his house again and shut the door.

I didn't see any of this. I was over the other side of the village working with some of the boyers from the other crews to get our tents ready for the camp. I heard the helicopter, but I thought it was the one the villagers used for checking the ice. It was only when I got back to Matulik's house for lunch that Dad filled me in on what had happened. He was brimming with excitement.

We sat with Matulik and Matulik's wife Leah for lunch in their kitchen. It wasn't as interesting as Turaq's kitchen – the curtains matched in that boring way – but I liked it anyway. It had a familiar feeling about it, even though we'd only been there a few days.

Matulik was still quivering with rage about the visit from the government man or whoever he was.

'You people,' he said to my dad, 'don' you got no manners? Comin' here like that, shouting orders to me.'

'Well…' said Dad.

I could see he wanted to assure Matulik it had nothing to do with us, but he didn't want to say anything that would make things worse.

'Sorry,' said Matulik then. 'I know it's nothing to do with

you. You're not from the government, right? Or the International Whaling Commission.'

'We're not even from the same *continent* as your government,' said Dad vehemently.

There was a silence for a while, except for the sound of knives and forks and people chewing quietly.

'So, what are you going to do?' Dad asked.

'Nothing,' said Matulik.

'You mean, you won't go out on the ice?'

'No, I mean do nothing different.'

'But the quota. What happens if you exceed the quota?'

'We don't exceed the quota. We never do. We agreed to the quota, we think it's right not to take too many whales – we've always known that.

'But we fix up the quotas between ourselves, see. We don't need a man in city shoes come in a helicopter to tell us. If the other villages have taken extra whales, they tell the folks at the main whaling centre, a few miles up along the coast, and they fix it so nobody takes any whales in the fall, that's all. It's not a *spring* quota, it's a year quota. We can even it out over the year, simple. We know how to manage these things.'

'I see,' said Dad. 'Well, that's good.'

'You people!' Matulik said, but he was saying it to himself, almost like a curse.

I didn't know then about all the conflict there'd been between people like us and people like Matulik, over whaling, over sealing, over trading, over prices for produce, over land. I hadn't a clue, really.

9

A Decision

I tackled my father later.

'Dad, what's all this about?'

'What's all what about?'

'The quota. A quota for what?'

'For whales. The people are only allowed to kill a certain number every year. It has to do with conserving the whales, so they don't die out like they almost did in the last century from over-exploitation, only of course that was by European whalers.'

Conserving, exploitation ... I hardly heard those words. Only one word leapt out at me from what my father said.

'Kill! Dad, do they *kill* the whales?'

My wonderful bowhead whales! I must have known. I must have known, but I'd been fooling myself. We'd been using words like 'whaling' and 'whale camp', all along, even 'taking whales'. But nobody'd actually used the word 'kill' before. Even so, surely I must have put two and two together. But I was so excited, so mesmerised by the splendour of these beasts that at last I was going to see, I didn't really allow myself to admit that this was all about hunting. About life and death, as my dad had said.

'Well, of course they do. What do you think they go whaling for?'

It felt as if the floor of my world had shifted and a hole had opened under my feet.

'Dad,' I said softly, 'I don't think I want to go on the hunt.'

'But we've come all this way! All the other boys are going. I thought you were so thrilled about it.'

I couldn't tell him I'd had some sort of naïve idea that I was just going whale-watching, like some tourist. 'Tourist' was a word my dad used like a swear word. So I pretended it was just that I'd changed my mind.

'Now that we're here,' I said, 'I don't think I could face it.'

Dad put a hand heavily on my shoulder.

'Well, I can't make you come if you don't want to,' he said. 'I know how you feel about the bowheads …'

He couldn't. He couldn't possibly know how I felt about the bowheads. Nobody could, because I'd never told anyone. In my head, they had become magical beasts, wondrous, enchanted creatures, creatures so magnificent and huge and powerful and venerable that it would be verging on murder to kill them.

'So think about it, OK?' Dad was saying.

I hadn't even been listening to whatever argument he was putting. The usual one about how whales aren't really so specially intelligent after all, probably, but that didn't matter to me, because my feelings about the bowheads were *feelings* – I had developed an emotional relationship with them, without ever having laid eyes on one of them, and it had nothing to do with whether they were intelligent or not, although I was sure they were, anyway.

The floor seemed to shift under me again, and again I fell. And this time the problem was that I knew I wanted to go on the hunt. I knew it, because as soon as I thought about not going, disappointment rose in my throat with a bitter taste. I was utterly confused. I wanted desperately to go, and yet I didn't want to have anything to do with whale-killing.

'OK,' I said, defeated. 'I'll think about it.'

But thinking about it didn't help. I'd been reading, studying, thinking, dreaming about bowhead whales for months now. They seemed to live boisterously inside my head, almost as if I'd invented them all by myself. My whole winter had been an anticipation of this trip. The more I thought about them, the more I longed to see them at last, the more confused I got, and the more torn between wanting to see the whales and not wanting to have anything to do with killing them.

I tried common sense. I said to myself that if I just made coffee and scared away polar bears, I wasn't really part of the killing team. I told myself that I'd come all this way, I was missing half a term at school, just for this, and I would be foolish to turn my back on it. I told myself that the whales were going to be killed anyway, whether or not I was part of it.

That was the trickiest bit to think about. If you can do nothing to prevent something you don't agree with, if it's going to happen anyway, well then, can you allow yourself to benefit from that thing? It was all so miserably confusing. In the end, I didn't so much decide as succumb.

'Made your mind up, son?' Dad asked me later.

I shook my head, feeling sickened inside, as if my thoughts were headaches, chasing each other around my skull.

Dad sat down beside me.

'OK,' he said, drawing up his chair closer to the table where I sat with my head in my hands. 'Let's try to think this through. Let's think for a minute about your sealskin parka.'

'I'm wearing it,' I said warily, half-aware where this argument was going to lead.

'Somebody had to kill a seal – several seals – to make it.'

'Yes,' I said. I had been right about where this argument was going.

I thought about seals, their sleek bodies, their innocent whiskery faces, their silly honking noises, the way they play on the rocks.

'I suppose nylon jackets could be just as good,' I said at last, reluctantly, though I knew from experience that it wasn't true.

'Well,' said Dad, 'that may or may not be true. But you know, nylon comes from oil.'

'Yes,' I said, wearily, 'which has to be mined from the earth, which creates environmental pollution and destroys communities.'

Damn! I thought.

'Plus it's a non-renewable resource. We get nothing for nothing in this world, you know.'

I shook my head. 'It's not the *same*,' I said.

'No,' he agreed. 'It's not. Animals are different. They're like us.'

He was changing sides! He saw it my way!

'That's it,' I said excitedly. 'That's the problem, Dad. They have *feelings*.'

'And then, apart from the skins,' Dad went on, 'there's the meat, which is probably even more valuable. Vegetarianism isn't really an option in the Arctic, you know. Not too many vegetable gardens around here. Meat is what you eat up here, or you die.'

He wasn't changing sides after all. He was just being reasonable. I looked around at the bleak snow-covered landscape, and I could see for myself he was right.

'But …' I said.

'And where do you get meat in a place like this?' Dad went on. I wished he would stop, but he kept on, relentlessly pursuing his argument. 'Not too many chicken farms round here either.'

'But …' I said again, lamely, casting about for some argument to throw at him, to stop him in his tracks.

'And it's not just us that live off dead animals,' he said. 'All of nature does. The whales themselves live off other sea creatures.'

'Plankton,' I said dully.

'Yes, bowheads eat plankton, but other whales eat fish. Octopus. Herring. It's how life works. We live off each other. The best we can do is to do it with a minimum of cruelty.'

His arguments were unanswerable.

'Shut up, Dad,' I said, covering my ears. 'Just shut *up*!'

I hate when the other person is right, and you know

they're right, and still you feel you were right all along too. It makes me feel woozy.

Give him his due, Dad did shut up. He closed his mouth firmly, in a thin line, and let me think.

I put my head in my hands again, covering my ears. The thoughts were crowding in on me, getting mixed up with the feelings. I could feel tears starting, but I didn't want to cry, not about whales, not in front of Dad.

'In the past ...' I said, after a bit, trying to work out what I thought.

'No,' said Dad, before I'd even got to the end of my sentence.

I wanted to biff Dad one, the way he was droning on with his clever arguments, interrupting me before I even got started, but we didn't go in for violence in my family, so I just kicked the leg of the table instead. Hard. My toe ached for ages afterwards.

'It doesn't matter whether it's the past or the present,' Dad was saying. 'The arctic people don't *have* to hunt for a living any more, but does that make their way of life suddenly wrong? So there are other meats, other oils, other materials – all of which have to be imported and paid for, by the way, all of which are bound up in their own moral issues too – but does that mean that the people should suddenly drop their way of life, change everything they have ever known and start living on fish fingers and wearing polyester?'

I was listening, but I felt glum inside, mixed up and sad and headachy and confused. I banged my fist on the table in frustration and anger.

'And anyway,' Dad went on, laying his hand over my

clenched fist to stop me banging it, 'what about the fish? How do you think they feel about having their fingers chopped off?'

'Oh Dad! That is such a *stupid* joke.'

I could feel tears spurting now from my eyes. Tears of anger, I told myself, pulling my fist out from under Dad's restraining hand and using it to dab fiercely at my wet face.

'Look, I'm trying to make the point,' Dad said, more gently now that he saw how upset I was, 'that everything we put in our mouths comes out of the earth or out of the sea, no matter how processed it is, no matter how far we try to remove ourselves from the way it was produced.'

'Shut up,' I said again, through clenched teeth.

I couldn't bear the way his logic and his arguments were sweeping over me, washing away my thoughts before I'd even formed them.

'OK,' said Dad, sitting back on his chair. 'Think about it for a while, son, but remember, we break trail tomorrow and I need to know if you are going to come with us or if you are going to stay at home with Leah.'

Matulik's wife wasn't going because she had arthritis and needed to keep warm.

'I don't want to think about it any more,' I said. 'Thinking is doing my head in. I'll come, OK? OK? I'll come!'

I didn't really want to go, but I couldn't imagine spending several days in a half-empty village trying to make small talk with Leah and the other old people, who would be staying at home to mind the youngest children, and a few other people who would have to stay in the village to keep the shop open and the generator running. Everyone else, all the village whaling crews, along with their wives and the older girls and boys, would have gone to the camp. That's really why I went in the end, because I couldn't decide to stay away. I wasn't proud of my decision, though.

Whaling

The next day, almost the whole village got ready to break trail to the place they were going to set up the whaling camp, near where the leads were in the ice. The ice doesn't break up conveniently close to the land. It's often twenty or thirty miles out to sea that the leads form, and the whaling crews have to travel out on the sea ice to wherever it is. Helicopters are very useful for spotting the best places, but there isn't room in a chopper for the whole crew, so they have to follow along on foot or by snowmobile, carrying all the camping and whaling equipment.

They call it breaking trail, and I began to see why. You do literally have to break a path for yourself across the ice. The pack ice is not all nice and flat and smooth. Very often big mounds of ice form, great towering, fabulous, glittering, crystalline banks of ice, like hard, sharp hills, and you have to break a way through these ice formations to create a path for the sleds and snowmobiles to get through. Breaking trail is hard work.

We were lucky. It was only a ten-mile journey to the place that had been chosen for the camp, and we were able to travel most of the way by snowmobile. It only took about a day to get from the village to the camping ground near where the ice had started to open up and make a channel through which the whales were already beginning to swim. Poor creatures, I thought, wishing I could warn them about their fate.

We struck camp that first night, the different crews spreading out along the ice, each crew forming its own little settlement, but all close by. As soon as we got the stuff unloaded to set up the camp, the girls and women started lighting camping stoves and getting food ready. Everyone was starving after the journey, and soon the delicious smell of fish cooking filled the air.

That was when I met Henry. He was about my own age or a little younger, short and thin and bouncy and very excited about being a boyer. He showed me how to cut a hole in the ice to make a sheltered place for the Primus stove.

'See, you put the ice you cut out of the hole around it like this, to make a little wall,' he explained – he was the chattiest Eskimo I ever met – 'to break the wind, and you put the stove in the hole, so it's sheltered.'

I nodded and watched as he lit the stove and set the coffee pot on it.

'Why can't girls be boyers?' I asked, mainly because I didn't want to think about the hunt.

Henry looked up from the blue flame of the stove and stared at me out of dark, puzzled eyes.

'Girls are girls,' he said eventually. 'Boys are boys. Only boys can be boyers.'

I didn't get it, so I asked again, why.

'Because,' said Henry, as if suddenly realising this for the first time, 'boys will grow up to be whalers, maybe even whaling captains.'

'And not girls?'

He looked at me as if I was totally mad.

'No,' he said, 'girls will be women,' as if that was something I couldn't work out for myself.

'And women can't be whalers?'

He laughed.

'How could they be?' he asked. 'They have their own work to do. If the women did the men's work, who would do the women's work?'

It seemed to have an undeniable logic to him. I didn't argue. I was the outsider, after all, and I didn't understand. In fact, as I now realise, the women play a very important role in the whaling – it's just that no one *thinks* of them as whalers.

It always seemed to smell of oil up north – diesel and seal oil, axle grease and engines. Modern life had hit the Arctic even then, and in the villages there were television sets and pool tables, deep-fat fryers and pickup trucks, but still every luxury was eked out at a cost, and everywhere was the oily stench of effort. Here at the camp, with snowmobiles parked around the edges of the settlement and everywhere bottled gas and oil-fired stoves, the greasy, oily, fumy reek, tinged with fish and sea, was even more intense than usual, a hard-working, basic smell that I will for ever associate with the Arctic.

When the tents were all up and the food was cooked, we sat around on anything we could find that was not ice to eat our supper. My dad and I sat in a snowmobile, which gave us some protection from the bitter arctic wind as well as from the freezing surface of the ice. They call it spring when the ice starts to break, but it's nothing like spring where I come from. No daffodils or tulips, that's for sure. It's just slightly less wintry, and the eternal night starts to move towards eternal day.

The whole crew ate together and laughed and told stories and danced, right through the long, slow sunset. You'd never think they were on a killing mission. It all seemed as innocent as a boy scouts' picnic.

Then, just as the air was turning that eerie silvery-navy colour that counted as night up there in the spring time, Matulik stood up and waved his arms for silence. Everyone stopped what they were doing and listened. We listened and listened in the deep blue air, our noses freezing, and the skin on our faces prickling with the cold. I pulled my sealskin parka around me, thinking of Turaq, wondering if he'd ever been a boyer with a whaling crew. I hoped he was OK, wherever he was.

And then we heard it. I seemed to feel it right inside my body, rather than just hear it, the way you can feel the percussion section in an orchestra if you sit close up. The steady rumble of movement in the water, the occasional splosh in the night and the grunts and clicks of concentration made by the bowhead whales pushing their way through the ice fields in the sea, just as we had pushed our way earlier through the piled up ice to get here. The bowhead is powerful enough to break its way through the hard-packed ice – I knew this from my pored-over library book – as long as it is not more than a foot or two thick, using its broad snout. We could hear loud creaks and tearing sounds as the ice was rent apart by the incessant onward progress of the whales. They weren't singing, as I'd half-expected they would be, just making their way warily and steadily under and through the ice, heading for the open seas.

At the sound of the whales, people moved on silent feet to douse the fires and to gather up their equipment. Usually the crews go whaling in the day time, when they are rested and can see what they are doing. But that evening the sound of the whales breaking into their suppertime revelry on the very first evening at camp had invigorated the whaling crews and they were suddenly all set for the hunt.

The women and girls withdrew like shadows into the tents. The boyers knotted together and the older lads gave whispered orders, telling us where to station ourselves to keep lookout. The men, meanwhile, were gathering up their equipment, all in this weird semi-silent near-darkness.

'Why has everything gone so quiet?' I asked Henry, who was on lookout with me near the edge of our camp.

'So as not to frighten the whales,' said Henry. 'We have to take them by surprise.'

The idea of not frightening the whales had a hollow ring to me. Don't alarm them – that way you can kill them easier.

Then there was a murmur from the men, a low, rhythmic sound in a strange language. It reminded me of the old people at home praying the rosary.

'What's that?' I asked Henry. 'What are they doing?'

'Speaking to the soul of the whale.'

'*What?*'

Henry sighed. 'Look, the whale is going to give itself up to the people. That is something very … umm … solemn.'

I stared at him, but he couldn't see the expression of complete puzzlement on my face in the dark. How come they could think the whale had a soul and still want to hunt it? I couldn't work it out. It all seemed wrong to me, wrong and wretched.

We sat and watched the men of our crew, visible, even though they were hundreds of yards away, as silent silhouettes against the blue-dark sky and the eerie gleam of the moonlit ice. They were dragging their skin-covered umiaq to the water's edge. They lowered it with a soft plop into the water and got noiselessly into it, each man swaying for a moment as he found his balance and then hunkering down and making room for the next crew member. The whaling equipment was already on board and ready to be used. I felt sick at the thought of it, the huge, heavy harpoon with its deadly spike, and the rifle looming in wait, in case the harpoon didn't succeed.

My dad didn't go in the boat with them. As an unskilled outsider, he would only have been a liability on the boat full of highly experienced whalers. He went instead and stood as close to the edge of the ice as he dared, and watched in the moonlight.

All along the edge of the ice, as far as we could see, umiaqs were lowered into the water, men slithered into the boats and swayed and steadied themselves. There were about five or six crews in all, I think, spread out along the ice, each with its own umiaq, each umiaq loaded with its own instruments of death.

Anticipation hung breathlessly in the darkening air as the

paddles plashed, turning streaks of silver out of the waters. The sound of the paddles carried on the cold, still air to where we squatted, watching, and the umiaqs slid off over the sea. We boyers glanced occasionally over our shoulders in a gesture of lookout, but really we were concentrating on what was happening just at the edge of our vision.

I was itching for a sight of the whales – poor, doomed creatures – but I daren't leave my post. Everyone had a job to do, and everyone in the crew depended on everyone else doing their job. Nobody had explained that to me, but I seemed to know it. I suppose I picked it up from the behaviour of the other boyers. They all did their tasks with such a grave air that I knew without thinking about it that we were vital, in our small way, to the success of the hunt. I didn't like that thought, but still, I had to play my part. I'd made my decision, I was there, I couldn't back out of it now.

I hunkered on the mat I'd brought with me from our tent to save my knees from contact with the icy floor and screwed up my eyes, desperate to see what was going on, wishing it wasn't going to happen, and yet bursting for it to be over with. I could hear the whales' low grunts and whistles, and I could picture their inky bodies, huge shadows in the icy seas. An occasional fount of whale-blow rose up on the horizon, silver-splashed in the moonlight, as a whale broke the surface for a breather, but mainly they moved quietly, under the surface, as if they knew we were watching and waiting.

Then suddenly, out of the stillness, a harpoon flew up with a heavy *whump* through the air. We could see – or imagined we could see – the cold arc of its lightning path against the sky, and then it hit its target with a solid thump, and immediately there was an explosion, an almighty crack in the murmurous silence of the night, like a train hitting a stone wall.

'What's that?' I whispered to Henry. 'What's that noise?' At least, I thought I was whispering, but I must have shouted to be heard over the terrible crash of the explosion.

The water was thrashing and boiling now with the stricken whale's sudden struggle, and his bellow roared over the water like a thunderbolt on wheels.

'The harpoon has a charge in it,' Henry said. 'It explodes when it hits the whale.'

'Oh my God!' I wailed. 'They *bomb* it!'

'It's so that the whale dies more quickly,' Henry explained. 'It's to prevent too much pain.'

The whale's dying call boomed out over the squealing rush of the other whales, bereaved, bewildered and panicking. I closed my eyes, and tried to stop my ears, torn between pity for the poor harpooned beast and terror that he would pull the whole fragile umiaq and crew down with him into the icy water in a last desperate dive for freedom. My heart felt squeezed in my chest as I heard, even through the fingers stuck hard in my ears, the whale's cry fading on the night air. I felt my heart expand then, as if daring to get pumping again only when the whale's last moment came. I opened my eyes and unstopped my ears, thankful at least not to have to hear the whale roaring in pain and contorting and twitching in the water.

Silence descended and hung for moments in the semi-darkness.

'Who got it?' I whispered to Henry then, meaning which of the crews.

'We did!' he said aloud, jubilation in his voice.

I wanted to kick him, to punch his grinning face in. I wanted to stamp my feet and pull my hood over my face and wail for the dead creature. But I just sat there and stared. Then, with shaking fingers, I struck a match and re-lit the stove we were in charge of. I warmed my fingers at the small flame and tried to think of nothing, nothing at all.

Sharing the Whale

Already the camp was alive with celebration. The women and girls emerged from the tents, carrying buckets and long knives and tarpaulins, and hurrying to the edge of the ice. The fishy, oily, metallic smell of whale and whale blood filled the air.

Matulik was already 'ashore' on the ice, and he and his crew members were working at an enormous winch they had set up as near as they dared to the edge of the ice. Members of other crews hurried to join them, to help with the work of bringing the whale ashore.

As the men worked, the sky started to pinken again, and all through the spreading blush of dawn Matulik's whaling crew and the other men worked the ropes and the winch and tackle. We boyers hurriedly cut lumps out of the ice with our snow knives, to melt down for water, and we made coffee on our little oil stoves for all we were worth. We took it in turn to run with cans of coffee to the edge of the ice and pour it steaming into mugs for the men as they worked.

They were glad of it, as much for the chance to warm

their hands, slippery with blood and ice and cold, as for the drink itself, and we were thrilled with the chance to get close to the action, even for a few moments.

We couldn't stand around for long, though, watching the men at their hauling and winching, for our job was still to man the camp and keep at bay any curious bears that might wander by, by banging saucepan lids and waving torches. Just because our crew had – miraculously – landed a whale on our very first night at camp, it was no excuse for us to leave our posts and gather round the catch.

All through the dawn the men worked, my dad among them, to raise the whale out of the water. The rising sun gilded their bodies, so that they looked, from our vantage point at the edge of the camp, like some sort of shining gods landed down on the ice to direct operations – rather squat gods, it has to be admitted, bundled in their hooded parkas and with their polar-bearskin leggings and long leather boots.

By the time the sun was high in the sky, the whale had been hauled out of the sea and lowered onto the ice bank and the butchering was about to begin. I ran forward, grabbing a coffee-pot as my excuse, to see the magnificent animal while it was still intact, with just a rivulet of blood running down from its huge, grimacing mouth, and congealing on the icy floor.

My eyes filled with unexpected tears. All these months bowheads had lived in my imagination, and now here I was looking at one for the first time – but it was dead. Sadness possessed me, and I turned away from the sight of the poor, destroyed beast.

'I'll have a swig,' said one of the men, thrusting an

enamel mug under the spout of my coffee pot.

I stared at him. It took a moment to register that he wanted coffee.

'Oh!' I said, and took the cup from him.

There was blood on the handle, but I grasped it firmly, to counteract the shake in my hand, and poured the coffee, black and acrid, and thrust it towards the whaler. Then I ran back to the camp, bashing my face with my arm as I ran, pretending I wasn't soaking up tears.

Children swarmed over the dead whale, now, singing and flinging their arms about, as if they had caught it themselves. Some of the mothers were taking photographs of the kids dancing on the whale, and the men were out with measuring tapes, trying to work out how long the whale was.

But soon the merrymaking had to let up because the work of the butchering had to begin. They cut a huge belt of meat from behind the head of the whale and divided it up into portions to be shared by the village families. This first cut of meat, from what they call the captain's belt, has to be given away. Everyone gets some except the whalers themselves.

'Why?' I asked Henry.

It seemed to me very odd to go to all that trouble to kill a whale and then give away the meat.

'Because that is the tradition,' Henry said.

'Yes, but why?'

'So that the whalers don't become greedy, I suppose,' he said. 'The whales are for everyone to share. If the whalers took the first meat for themselves, then they would not be sharing. The sharing is the important thing. That's how our people have always survived. If we didn't share, we died.'

'Oh,' I said. 'I didn't know that.'

That cheered me up a bit.

Soon the chief boyer came by and sent me and Henry to bed. We'd been up all night, though I'd hardly noticed, there'd been so much happening. Now it was the turn of the younger boyers, who had been sent to bed at sunset, to get up and take their turn at the boyers' work.

It was only when I finally climbed into my sleeping bag that I realised how exhausted I was. It had been a long, exciting, confusing, distressing day and night, and now I needed desperately to sleep. The last thing I thought as I drifted off was that I hoped the younger boyers would be as efficient as we were at scaring off the polar bears. That bloody smell in the air would be sure to attract them.

12

The Igloo

The polar bears held off. I don't know whether it was good luck or the good efforts of the other boyers. Or maybe there were no polar bears at all in that area. Maybe the grown-ups just wanted us to feel important.

I woke up feeling stiff and giddy. I rubbed my eyes with my hands and smelt the smell of stale blood. I looked at my hands. My left hand was smeared still with the dried blood of the whale, which I had picked up off the coffee mug of the whaler I had served. I shuddered. I was implicated in this butchery, whether I liked it or not.

Outside, an impromptu feast was going on. The whalers had taken a break from their butchering work and the women had set up stoves beside the whale and were cooking maktak.

'What's that?' I asked.

'Whale skin,' said Matulik, handing me a piece. 'It's delicious. You should try some, Tyke.'

I stepped back.

'No,' I said, horrified at the idea of eating boiled whale skin. 'Anyway, I thought you had to give it away to people not in the crew.'

'Well, you're a guest,' said Matulik, licking his fingers. 'But anyway, this is maktak, it's the skin, not the meat. My favourite. You sure you don' want some?'

But I drew the line at actually eating the whale.

The rest of the day was spent in feasting and celebrating, but also in working. The whale had to be divided up into pieces for distributing to all the village families and for storing in icy cellars, so it could be eaten later in the year. There were several days' work in that, and even though they had been up all night catching the whale, the crew worked hard all day dealing with their giant catch, the men cutting and butchering, the women packing and labelling. They took it in turns to slip away for a couple of hours' sleep, but the work never stopped. Meanwhile, Henry and I were back on coffee-duty, and we were kept busy running around the crew with steaming cups.

Matulik and the captains of the other crews had had a meeting, and decided not to stay at the camp and try for a second whale. They were happy with their catch and they didn't want to run into trouble with the quota people. Some men from the other crews came to help with the butchering. The others set off back to the village to bring news of the success of the hunt and to pass on the message to the neighbouring villages that Matulik's crew had caught a whale and that none of the village crews would hunt any more, because of the quota. This was in the days before mobile phones, of course.

Meanwhile, a member of one of the other crews was

building a snow house.

'Oh, an igloo!' I said, remembering 'I is for igloo' from my alphabet book when I was small. E is for Eskimo, I thought. And U is for unicorn. Crazy words those alphabet people used, I thought. Xylophone. Yak. Zebra.

'Yes,' said Henry. 'Isaac is the last person in the village to know how to do it properly, like in the old days. We don't use snow houses much any more, but Isaac likes to build them, and we can use this one to store the whale meat till we're ready to go back to the village.'

We watched from our coffee-station as Isaac worked, cutting blocks of frozen snow right out of the landscape and shaping them with his snow knife. He worked alone for most of the day, but occasionally other men came and helped. By evening, he had made a beautiful dome-shaped house with a long, low entrance-crawl.

Henry asked him if we could go inside.

'Well, jus' for a moment,' Isaac said, 'but don' go foolin' aroun', this here's meant for the whale meat, not for boy-ers.'

'We just want to take a look,' said Henry.

'And don' go *breathin'* in there!' Isaac warned us. 'You'll heaten it up if you do.'

'Does he expect us to hold our breaths?' I asked Henry.

He laughed. 'Not really,' he said. 'He just means not to spend too long in there. Snow houses get very warm once there are people inside for any length of time. But he wants it to be cold, to keep the meat in.'

'Why not just leave it lying around in the snow, then?' I asked.

Henry looked at me once again as if I was mad.

'You want every polar bear in the country to come by and eat our catch?'

'Oh, yeah, the bears,' I said, sheepishly.

We wriggled into the snow house on our stomachs. It was cold in the entrance-crawl, and cold inside, just like being in a fridge, and dark too. But it was very still, because we were suddenly sheltered from the endless arctic wind and after a while, being out of the wind, it began to feel quite balmy, in comparison with the constant chill outside. We were insulated from the noise of the butchering also. It was a bit like being in a low, icy cave.

'You have to imagine a lamp, see,' said Henry's voice out of the icy darkness. 'A whale-oil lamp or a seal-oil lamp.'

'Yes,' I said, 'because there's no window.'

'But mainly for heat,' said Henry.

'For heat? A lamp for heat?'

'Yes, in a snow house, an oil-lamp gives out enough heat to make it really snug.'

'My,' I said.

'I know a story about an igloo,' Henry said. 'You want to hear it?'

I didn't know then that Henry was beginning to earn a reputation as the village storyteller. I suppose that's the skill he developed in later years when he took up journalism.

I didn't really want to hear Henry's story. I wanted to get out of that cold, eerie little building. But I thought I'd better listen. It was the sort of thing my dad would probably want to know, so I said, 'OK.'

'There was a real bad hunter, see,' said Henry's voice out of the dark. 'He never managed to catch any game. One day when he was out looking for something to hunt, he spotted a polar bear and he crawled over the ice to try and get it. But the bear said, "Don't shoot me. If you spare my life and do as I say, I will make you a great hunter."

'The bear told the man to climb on his back and close his eyes, and then the bear dived down into the sea, with the hunter on his back, down, down, down into the depths.

'Then they swam back up again, and landed on another shore, where there was an igloo at the edge of the ice. Inside the igloo was another bear with a spear stuck into his haunch. The first bear said, "If you take that spear out of my friend, you will become a good hunter." And so the hunter broke off the shaft and eased the spear point out of the bear's haunch.

'Then the first bear took off his bearskin parka and turned into a man. After the other bear's wound was healed, the bear-man put back on his bearskin parka, told the poor hunter to climb on his back and close his eyes, and back they went down into the sea again.

'When they came out of the sea and the hunter opened his eyes, he was back where he had started from. And from that day on, the man was always a good hunter.'

'Hey, I've heard a story like that,' I said, 'only it was a deer, not a bear.'

'An Irish story?'

'Yes.'

'Do your people hunt?'

'Not any more,' I said. 'In the past, I suppose, they hunted deer for food. But nowadays, we don't believe in hunting in Ireland.'

'What do you mean, you don't believe in it?' asked Henry.

'I mean, we don't like to kill wild animals.'

What a whopper! I'd very conveniently omitted to mention fox-hunting.

'Only tame ones? Like, pets? Animals you *know*?' Henry sounded shocked.

'Well, farm animals,' I said. 'It's not the same.'

'Hmm,' said Henry. 'I don't see that.'

I felt uncomfortable, as if I was lying. I wasn't exactly, but I wasn't being honest either. We were all in this killing business together, but I wasn't prepared to admit it.

'It's wrong to kill whales,' I said sanctimoniously.

'Why?' Henry sounded completely mystified.

'Whales have families. They love each other.'

'All animals have families,' said Henry. 'All creatures love their young. But we gotta live.'

I hated Henry then, just as I'd resented my father, for being right. But I didn't have the energy to fight, so I changed the subject.

'Let's get out, Henry. We're breathing too much.'

'Right,' said Henry. 'And we have to get after them polar bears.'

'Yeah,' I said. 'Let's go.'

13

Henry Goes Missing

After a few days, when the poor old whale had been completely dissected, and even the bones had been disassembled and packed up, we got ready to break camp and set off back to the village. There was even more commotion making ready to go home than there had been on the way out to the camp, because the people were jubilant at their success, and their busyness was infused with joy.

I never noticed that Henry was missing, not for ages. I was too busy helping to pack and chattering to my dad about the hunt. But just as we were loading our tents onto the snowmobile, I realised I hadn't seen him for hours. Was he avoiding me? I wondered. Was he annoyed at what I'd said about killing whales?

'I bet he's in the snow house,' I said to Dad. 'He really likes it in there.'

'But the snow house is full of whale meat,' said Dad.

'No. It's been packed up for going home,' I said. 'It'll be empty again by now.'

'Well, but it'll smell of whale, it'll be bloody and greasy. I can't imagine him going in there just to play.'

Play! Really, adults haven't got a clue, have they? If Henry had gone into the snow house, it would be because he liked it in there. He wouldn't be playing house!

Anyway, we went looking for him, me and my dad, but he wasn't in the snow house. I crawled in, and Dad was right, it stank in there, but there was no sign of Henry.

'Would he have gone on ahead with one of the other crews?' Dad suggested.

'No, I don't think so,' I said. 'He's very responsible about being a boyer. He'd never just go off home and not say. Anyway, his dad is part of this crew and his older brother. He'd hardly want to go home with a different family, would he? Dad?'

Dad grunted.

'You don't suppose a polar bear got him, do you?' I still wasn't sure if there really were polar bears about, but I didn't like the thought of them all the same.

'No! I don't suppose so, not for a minute.'

'Well, they keep going on about bears.'

'Yes, but if a bear came to the camp, we'd know all about it. We'd hear it, see it, there'd be tracks. A bear couldn't just happen by and run off with a boyer and nobody notice.'

'You sure?' I asked.

'Of course I'm sure,' said Dad.

But I thought he was being too light-hearted. If polar bears weren't such a danger, why would the people keep talking about them? I was worried about my friend, and starting to feel a bit guilty too that maybe I'd driven him away with my talk about whale-hunting being so dreadful. This was very unlikely, I see that now. You wouldn't get rid of Henry that easily. But at the time I was worried and confused. You think daft things when you're anxious.

'Look,' said Dad, 'you keep looking around here. I'll go around the other camps and see if he's gone to visit a friend. But I won't say anything to his dad yet. Don't want to worry him. If we don't find him within the hour, we'll meet back at our tent, and decide what to do. OK?'

'OK,' I said, but really it didn't seem a very good plan to me. I couldn't imagine any place else he could be, apart from in the snow house. There were no trees, no walls, no ditches to hide in. Nothing but snow and ice and sea and emptiness.

14

Tyke to the Rescue

I wandered off along what we thought of as the shore, but was really the point where the frozen sea met the watery sea. I was further up the coast, a bit away from the spot where the whale had been landed and the big clean-up operation was going on. I could hear the murmur of work and the occasional shout on the air, but I was pretty much out of actual earshot. All I could see of the villagers, when I looked over my shoulder, was constant movement up and down the icy shoreline as men and boys and girls and women moved about, packing and readying themselves for the homeward journey.

In one direction, the ice stretched in a glaring white expanse for miles and miles. It was enough to give you a headache looking at it, there was so much gleaming, retina-stretching white. In the other direction was the indigo expanse of the ocean. Since it was spring and the ice was breaking up, small sections of the icy shore were constantly breaking off and drifting out to sea, so that the surface of the water was dotted with the glittering debris of the break-up, little flat ice islands and odd half-melted lumps of ice like tiny icebergs jostling their way along, bumping off each other, drifting together sometimes, and then floating off again.

Overhead the sky was the bluest blue you can imagine, an icy, terrifying blue, far bluer than the skies you see in hot places, and streaked with feathery white cloud on the horizon. There was so much ice and so much sea, so much white and so much blue, that I thought we'd never find Henry. You could walk for miles on the icy shore, calling his name, and all you'd see would be blue and white and white and blue, broken only by the huge inky shapes of the bowheads flickering through the sea like giant shadows, making large dark zeppelins under the surface, with an occasional dark shape drifting elephantinely to the surface, its blow erupting through the deep blue water into silvery fountains.

I walked the endless ice away from the noise and the bustle of the camp and the stench of food and blood and oil and into the icy blue wilderness. I concentrated on Henry, imagining that if I thought hard enough about him, I could conjure up an image of where he was in my head.

Every now and then, I scanned the horizon, pointlessly as I thought, but then something seemed to flutter on one of the drifting ice floes way out to sea. I screwed up my eyes and sure enough, the flutter came again. Someone was moving about, waving, on one of the drifting ice floes. It had to be Henry. I waved back, throwing all my strength into the movement of my arms, to assure him that I'd seen him.

I turned then and yelled for my dad. I yelled and yelled

till my throat hurt, but it was several minutes since he'd left. He'd evidently walked out of earshot by now. I started to run in the direction he'd gone, but then I stopped. It could take me ages to catch him. By then Henry might have floated off out of sight, and I'd never find him in the huge, heaving expanse of sea and float-ice.

If I'd had time to think I'd never have done it, but I was in such a panic my body acted on its own. There were umiaqs everywhere about. I leapt into one, loosely tethered to a grappling iron driven into the ice. I undid the rope that held it, and pushed it away from the ice shore. It was only after I'd got it out on the water that I thought to look for oars. The boat was full of things – a small stove, a harpoon, a gun and, thank heavens, paddles.

I'd never rowed even a little rowing boat, much less manned a boat of this size, heavy with equipment, across an expanse of arctic sea, bobbing with ice islands, but somehow I managed to get it moving roughly in the direction I wanted it to go. I kept my eyes fixed on Henry's drifting ice floe. He was yelling to me. I could hear his cries floating on the icy air, but I couldn't hear what he was trying to tell me. I knew I had to reach him. I had to. If I didn't rescue him, he could go floating off and over the horizon and never be heard of again. It happens to arctic hunters all the time, one of the hazards of their way of life.

'I'm coming!' I yelled, but I knew he couldn't possibly hear me. Still, it helped to shout it. It kept me going.

I paddled and paddled, but I didn't seem to be getting any closer. Was I going around in circles? I thought I must be, because I was only paddling on one side. I grabbed another paddle and tried to use them like oars, but the boat was too wide for me. I couldn't reach across it to use two paddles at once.

I stood up and paddled frantically from one side, then, unsteadily, I slithered to the other side of the boat and paddled a bit more on that side. Slowly, slowly, the boat moved in wide arcs. It wasn't exactly going in circles, but it was zigzagging forward only very slowly. Most of the movement was sideways, in the sweep of the arcs. I could see this was a problem, but it was the only way I could make the umiaq move at all, so I kept paddling, wriggling from one side to the other and paddling, paddling, paddling furiously.

Every now and then, I looked up to check if I could still see Henry. Every time I looked, he seemed further away, but I could hear his panic-stricken cries and I kept heading for him, though I was getting exhausted.

At last – it seemed like hours – I started to get closer. Each time I looked up, he seemed a little larger, a little easier to make out. I came close enough to hear his voice, as distinct from just yells, to hear actual words. He was shouting directions. He stood on the edge of his ice floe, which was bobbing along with slow, almost dreamy movements on the swell of the sea, and yelled instructions at me. He understood boats better than I did, so I listened.

'Paddle from the left,' he was shouting. 'Keep going. OK now, quickly, from the right. Quick, quick, she's circling, stop her! Good, good, now a few more goes on the right. Now run to the other side ...'

Slowly, slowly, the boat swung closer and closer to Henry's ice floe, but every time we were about to make contact, the ice floe drifted tantalisingly away again. It was like trying to catch an ice cube in a sink with wet fingers. I can't, I thought. I can't do it. I'm too tired. It won't do what I want.

'Just keep coming,' yelled Henry. 'You are getting closer. You are. Just don't lose your nerve, don't panic and don't tire.'

My arms were taut as iron rods by now with the effort of paddling, and the constant evasive action of the ice floe was beginning to wear me down, but Henry's shouts kept me concentrated on what I was doing.

Eventually, I felt the umiaq make contact with the ice with a gentle bump. The mild impact propelled the boat back again, but with the next paddle we made contact again, like a currach nosing in to a harbour wall. On the third impact, Henry's outstretched arm brushed mine, and on the fourth attempt, he took a flying, floundering leap and landed in the umiaq like a huge, thrashing fish. The boat rocked dangerously with the impact, and hit off the ice floe several times, but I steadied it by bracing my feet against the sides, and gradually it settled on the water.

Henry scrambled off the floor and, keeping his body bent to prevent overturning the boat, he managed to sit down.

'Hey, Henry!'

He looked smaller than himself, and his body was shaking, shaking, his face white and thin.

'Hey, Tyke!' he said, his voice wobbly and small. He looked as if he was trying to smile, but he couldn't manage it.

He leaned over the side of the boat then and projected a stream of vomit out over the sea.

I stared at him, listening helplessly to his retching. It was only when I saw him getting sick that I realised how close he'd been to death, how scared he must have been. I started to feel scared myself, then – up to then I'd felt only panic and unnamed terror, but now it was real, logical, believable fear, fear of death, fear of drowning, fear of never seeing my dad again. Mum, I thought suddenly. Oh, Mum! I felt bile rise in own throat. I swallowed hard and looked away, determined not to join Henry in getting sick. Somebody had to keep upright, and it would have to be me.

Henry turned to me then, still half-hanging over the side of the boat, vomit-streaked snot hanging from his nose, and I could feel the shaking of his body rocking the boat.

'Here,' I said, and I threw a hanky at him. 'Wipe up.'

He wiped his streaming face with the handkerchief and then he held it out to me.

'Yuck!' I said, and pulled away from it.

'Oh, sorry,' he said with half a smile.

He trailed the hanky in the water, wrung it out and wiped his face with it again. He bunched the wet hanky up then and threw it in the bottom of the boat.

'That's better,' Henry said, and picked up a paddle.

'You OK?' I asked.

'I'll live,' he said and leant over the side of the boat to help me manoeuvre it away from the ice floe. We paddled furiously, but without co-ordination, and so instead of moving the boat away from the island, we rammed it back against the edge of the ice with double-force, and, with a sickening scrunch, the prow of the boat wedged itself into a crevice in the ice and we were stuck fast.

Henry pushed against the ice with his paddle, but the boat wouldn't budge. I leant over and we both pushed and heaved with all our might, but we didn't have much strength left between us, and the umiaq had embedded itself in the ice. It wouldn't give an inch.

'What'll we do?' I wailed. My teeth were chattering now, with fear as much as cold, and my body was shaking from the efforts I was making to shift the boat.

'One of us is going to have to get off the umiaq and back onto the ice floe,' said Henry, 'and use the paddle to lever the boat away from the ice.'

'Not me,' I said quickly. I knew my own limits. I'd probably slip, I'd probably fall into the water, I'd probably die. I knew what a spill into the arctic waters could do. I could feel the pain of the freezing water gripping my limbs without so much as a splash getting on my skin.

'Me then,' said Henry.

I stared at him, and he stared back. I couldn't see how he was going to muster either the strength or the courage to get back off the boat, having just made it aboard. I'd have cowered in the boat and refused to move.

'But it's moving!' My voice was thin and high with anxiety. I couldn't believe this was happening to us, that my dad and Henry's dad were less than a quarter of a mile away and here we were going to be lost at sea.

'Yup,' said Henry, his eyes scrunched up in concentration. 'Still, that's the only way we can get the umiaq loose. Otherwise we're going to drift off all the way to the North Pole.'

Something about the idea of the North Pole froze my heart. I imagined a maypole, spiralling red and white like a barber's pole, and me and Henry slumped at the bottom of it, waiting for a polar bear to come along and gobble us both up.

Henry stood up unsteadily and then, with a sudden spurt of energy, he leapt off the boat and back onto the ice floe. He stood on the ice floe again and kicked the edge of the umiaq with all his force. Nothing happened. He kicked again and again, and then he prised his paddle into the crevice and at last, with a groan, the boat released itself and bobbed out, away from the ice. Henry took another flying leap and landed in the boat as it floated away. There was another awful moment as the boat rocked and rocked and rocked, steadying itself from the impact of Henry's leap, but it settled as it had before. Henry lay slumped against the side of the boat for a while, gathering his strength.

'You OK?' I asked again.

He nodded wearily, then sat up straight and picked up a paddle.

With two of us paddling, the umiaq moved more swiftly and in a perceptible direction. I felt my heart begin to lift as the shore came closer. We were going to survive. It was only when I thought that, that I fully realised how close we had come to not surviving. I looked at Henry, and he was looking at me.

'Hey, Henry,' I said again.

'Hey, Tyke,' he said and grinned.

But we weren't home yet. We still had an expanse of water to cross, with only a flimsy boat between us and the freezing ocean. We paddled away for a bit, saying nothing, concentrating on keeping the boat moving.

I looked over the edge into the water and thought about how many miles down it was to the depthless bottom and how many tons of water were under the boat, and as I looked, a shadow nudged by, a huge, huge shadow, like a submarine only much swifter and more graceful.

'Henry,' I said, in as low a voice as I thought he could hear. 'There's a whale on this side of the boat. It's close enough to touch.'

I remember thinking as I said that, that this was the realisation of my dreams, to be within touching distance of a bowhead whale. I never thought I ever would be, and I certainly never thought that if I was, I would be alone on the ocean with another boy in a skin boat and in danger of being capsized at any moment by a casual flick of the whale's tail.

'Hmm,' said Henry, his voice also low, hardly more than a whisper, 'there's one on this side too. But whatever you do, don't touch it, Tyke. Pull your paddle in.'

I didn't need to be told a second time. I drew my paddle in as calmly and quietly as I could, and we both sat huddled together, our paddles dripping ice-cold sea-water onto the flat floor of the boat. We sat silently, drifting casually, like two people out for a little leisurely boating and taking a break from the hard work of making the craft move, but knowing that we were in danger of being flicked over at any moment. Even if we didn't drown, we would probably die of hypothermia if we hit the water and down our bodies would go, cold and twirling, to the bottom of the sea. I shuddered at the thought.

We practically held our breaths, allowing the air to escape from our bodies only very slowly and quietly, desperate to make ourselves invisible, inaudible, not there. Occasionally a whale breached, its huge body suddenly ungainly out of the water, lumbering as a hippopotamus. One whale let out its giant blow so close that we were both drenched in the warm, salty, fishy mist of its breath, and we could hear its soft whining calls, as if it was talking, complaining, to itself. But still we sat motionless in our boat, and waited for all the whales to swim by.

They kept coming, pod after pod of them, with short gaps in between, swishing and flickering, always avoiding the boat, though they swam very near to it. It was as if they were aware it was there, and they were swimming around the obstruction it caused on the surface. We could see the swift movements of their tails as they swam, displacing the water and propelling them forward, and occasionally we saw a whale nose an ice floe out of the way.

Still they came, and still we sat, and the sky started to get that flushed look I now knew was the beginning of the sunset. My shoulders ached, partly with the effort of paddling, but mostly with the effort of sitting still. My feet were like two overgrown ice cubes slithering about in the bilge-water on the floor of the boat. And still we sat and still the whales swam by.

At last, they passed on, but even after we ceased to see the great underwater shadows and to hear their whines and soft screeches, we sat still for a long time, just in case, in the air that seemed to reverberate with the whales' yearning hoots even after they'd swum out of earshot.

Henry shifted beside me and expelled a long, sighing outbreath. He stretched then and picked up his paddle. I did the same, and soon we were moving to the shore again, our aching limbs urging the boat forward as the sky deepened.

'Wasn't that ...' I cast about for a word. 'Scary' came to mind, but although it had been scary, that wasn't the word I wanted. '... weird?' I finished, though 'weird' wasn't really the word I wanted either.

'Weird,' said Henry. 'Almost … what's that word? Mystical.'

A little shiver went through me when he said it. That was the word I'd wanted, but I'd probably have been embarrassed to say it even if I could have thought of it.

I nodded, but then the spell was broken and I laughed. It was all too much, and we needed to break the terrible tension.

'Verrry myshticle,' I said, exaggerating my Irish accent. 'Verry, verry myshticle indeed. That was a very myshticle shower of whale blow, wasn't it. Myshticle and mishty, ahh!'

Henry laughed too and his shoulders shook.

We laughed, but then we were only boys. We didn't know how to talk about it, but we knew it was true. It *had* been mystical.

We paddled on for a bit, and then I said: 'I wouldn't blame them if they'd killed us.'

'Who?' asked Henry.

'The whales.'

'Why would they want to kill us?'

'Because we killed one of them.'

'Yes, but that was a hunt,' said Henry. 'We didn't kill the whale out of anger.'

'What difference does that make? You kill it, it's dead.'

'All the difference. If we were fighting the whales, if we were killing them for fun or because we wanted to get rid of them, then they would be angry. But when we hunt, we pray for the whale, we ask the whale to give itself up to feed the people. We release its spirit. There's no need for anger.

That's just how things are. The whales know that.'

He sounded very sure of himself, but I couldn't agree. How could the whales know a thing like that? It didn't make any sense. And I noticed that for all his talk, Henry had been just as anxious as I was not to disturb the whales when they swam near our boat. But I didn't argue. I just kept paddling.

'Like the bear in the story,' Henry added.

'What?'

'The bear in the story. The story is about how the people and the animals help each other.'

Yes, but that's a fairytale, I thought to myself, but I didn't say so out loud.

We made much better progress with the umiaq now that there were two of us and pretty soon the ice shore seemed reachable. There were figures standing about on the ice, watching us. They seemed to be getting umiaqs ready to come out to meet us, but I think when they saw that we were making good progress, they held back. As we came closer, I saw that two of the people were my dad and Henry's dad and they had a pair of binoculars that they kept passing from one to the other. When they could see us getting closer, they started punching each other encouragingly on the upper arms and hallooing and roaring and waving their arms at us.

'How on earth did you manage an umiaq on your own?' asked Dad, as he put out his hand to help me ashore.

'I have … absolutely … no idea,' I said, putting my foot on 'dry land'. The words came out like washing from a wringer, all stretched and squeezed. It seemed to hurt my chest to talk.

That's the last thing I remember, my dad's hand under my elbow and my feet touching the pack ice. My dad said I collapsed at his feet. Exhaustion, he said. I don't think so. I think it was sheer relief.

15

The Whale Feast

I don't remember the next bit, because I was out of it, but Dad and Henry told me what happened. I went all floppy, Dad said, so they had to give me brandy – they forced it between my lips – and make a stretcher out of whale bones and sleeping bags and put me on it and drag me back over the ice, semi-conscious and hallucinating, on a sled. But I recovered pretty quickly once I got warmed up and got something to eat and drink.

Now I was sitting up in bed, wriggling my toes in a pair of deliciously warm furry socks Leah had made me put on.

'Dad,' I said, 'Mum …'

'… doesn't need to hear about this, right?'

'Right. It would only …'

'… worry her, I know.'

It didn't strike me at the time, but Dad was just as quick to hide my adventures from Mum as I was. Maybe he thought she'd think he wasn't looking after me properly.

'Well,' Dad said then, 'I think Turaq would be proud of you.'

'Turaq?' I said groggily.

'Turaq. Remember Turaq?'

'Of course I remember Turaq. The guy with the parka. Said nothing much. Saved my life.'

'That's right,' said Dad. 'Like you saved Henry's.'

I thought for a while about that. It sounded very grand.

'Did I?'

'Of course you did.' Dad beamed at me and gave me a quick hug, quick enough so I couldn't squirm out of it. 'You saved his life, and you risked your own life to do it. You were very brave.'

Brave? Me? Brave? Maybe I was, I thought, maybe I had saved Henry's life. Yes, I suppose I must have. You did hear stories about hunters being taken out to sea on break-off ice floes and never being heard of again. I was glad that hadn't happened to Henry. I liked him.

'So it's like what Turaq's grandma said,' I said.

'Exactly,' Dad agreed.

Henry told us later what had happened. He'd gone walking close to the edge of the ice and he'd got engrossed in watching some whales out to sea, and before he knew it, the section of the ice he was standing on broke away and floated off out across the water. He thought at first he might leap off and make it to the shore, but suddenly the channel between him and the shore widened, and he had no chance of jumping. He thought about swimming, but he figured water would be dangerously cold. He knew how quickly hypothermia could set in. So, while he dithered about what to do, the ice floe got caught in a current and picked up speed, and before he knew it, he was practically out to the open sea.

'I don' know,' Henry said in his droll way when he called by to visit. '*I'm* the one got stranded on the ice floe and *you're* the one gettin' all the attention. What you gotta do to get noticed round here? – Oh, I know. Collapse.'

'No,' I said indignantly. 'You've got to be a hero.'

'Oh, so you a hero, then?'

'Of course I am,' I said. 'Tiger Tyke the Life-Saver, that's me!'

'Well, I suppose I have to admit you did save my life. You can call that being a hero if you like. Some people think the village'd be better off without dreamers like me.'

'Are you fishing for compliments?' I asked, 'or are you just running yourself down to make out I'm not a hero?'

'Umm,' said Henry. 'I'm not sure. But if it makes you feel better, thanks for saving my life.'

'You don't sound very sincere,' I said.

'What you want, I gotta lick your mukluks?'

'No. Just make me a nice cup of tea, maybe.'

'You and your tea! You're a tea-addict, you know that? But OK, life-saver, only then you get up. We're going to have the whale feast soon. You can't miss that.'

The whale feast happened after the whaling crews all came home and the meat was distributed, first among the villagers in general, and then among the crew that took the whale. Every family got enough so they had meat to put in the ice for eating in the winter when food was scarcer. But not all the meat was stored for later. Some of it was eaten fresh, at the whale feast, which was held in Matulik's house, because it was Matulik's crew that caught the whale. I was still feeling bad about the poor bowhead whale, and I'd rather not have gone to the whale feast, but I didn't really have a choice. It was pretty unavoidable, given that we were living in Matulik's house.

I have to admit that I did try just a little of the meat at the feast, but I didn't like it. The local people all thought it was the most delicious thing they'd ever eaten. They ate every bit of it, even the blubber. I felt ill looking at the greyish-yellowish wobbly stuff. They laughed at me for not liking it, but I was kind of glad that I didn't enjoy it. I felt it was more principled of me not to like whale meat, considering how I felt about the whales.

16

The Story of Sedna

Dad got talking to Henry. He'd found out that Henry was well known in the village for his stories. Henry's grandfather had told him some of the old tales and a lot about the old way of life, before he died, and he'd told Henry it was up to him to remember, so that the next generation of people would still have the stories. To me it was pretty obvious why the grandfather had told the stories to Henry – because he was the biggest chatterbox this side of the Arctic Circle, and so it was a good bet that he'd pass the stories on.

Dad said the stories Henry had were already known to anthropologists, but he said he was still interested in hearing Henry's versions of them and talking to him about what he thought the stories meant. So when Henry said, one day after the whale feast, that he wanted to tell me the most important story about whales and whaling, I asked if I could call Dad.

It was evening time, and I'd already gone to bed when

Henry called round, but I wasn't asleep. So Henry sat at the foot of my bed and said he'd tell me his story, since I was all tucked in for the night.

Henry was delighted when I said I wanted Dad to hear the story too, though he pretended not to be. He said, 'Aw, if you have to,' when I asked, but I could see that his mouth had turned up at the ends. He couldn't hide it. So I yelled for Dad, and Dad came in and sat on his bed, which was a campbed and lower down than mine – I had the proper bed, belonging to Matulik's son – and we both listened.

'Once there was a beautiful girl called Sedna,' said Henry. 'She lived with her father, and she was old enough to be married, but she didn't fancy any of the young men who came to woo her. She thought she was too beautiful for them. She was waiting for an exceptionally handsome young lover to come and claim her, but he never came.'

I giggled at this bit, and Henry glowered, so I sobered up and listened.

'Time and time again she turned down the men who came to her camp wishing to marry her. In the end, her father got tired of her choosiness. It was time she had a husband. They were running out of food, and if she didn't find a husband to take care of her, they were going to die of hunger. So he decided that he would make her marry the next man who came looking for her. Sedna just brushed her beautiful long, midnight-black hair and ignored her father.

'Soon her father saw a man approaching their camp. He was dressed in fabulous, wealthy-looking furs, with his rich, furry hood drawn right up around his face. Here was just the man for his daughter, Sedna's father thought, so he offered Sedna to the wealthy-looking man.

'"She is beautiful," he assured him, "and she is a good worker. She can cook and sew and she will make a good wife."

'Sedna did not want to marry the stranger, but her father put her aboard the stranger's kayak and off they went to the stranger's country.

'Soon they arrived at a barren island. There was no house or hut to live in, not even a tent, just bare rocks and a cliff. Sedna's new husband stood in front of her and, letting out an evil laugh, he pulled down his hood to reveal his face. It was not a man at all, but a giant raven in disguise.

'Sedna screamed in terror and tried to run away from him, but the raven dragged her to a ledge on a cliff, where she was going to have to live like a bird. There was nothing on the hard, cold rocky ledge but a few feathers and a few tufts of hair. This was where she was supposed to make her home.

'There was nothing to eat, so the raven went in search of food. After a day and a night, he came back to Sedna on her rocky outcrop and dropped a raw fish into her lap.

'Sedna cried and cried and called for her father, and through the howling arctic winds Sedna's father heard his daughter's cries. He realised that he had made a mistake and he decided he had better come and rescue her. So he loaded up his kayak and paddled for days through the frigid arctic waters to the island, where Sedna stood waiting for him on the shore.

'Sedna was relieved to see her father, and she immediately jumped into his kayak and off they paddled, back towards home. But while they were out on the sea, Sedna spotted a black speck far off in the distance. She knew at once that it was the raven and that he was coming to get her.

'Sure enough, the raven got closer and closer and they could see his angry beak snapping. He swooped down on the kayak bobbing on the ocean, and Sedna's father struck out at him, using his paddle, but the big angry black bird dodged his blows and pecked and snapped at them.

'Then the raven flew with a swoop over the kayak and flapped his wings menacingly, calling up a storm, and almost immediately the wind began to blow viciously and the rain and hail lashed down on Sedna and her father, out at sea in the little kayak. The sea raged around them and tossed the fragile boat on the waves.

'Sedna's father was seized with a terrible fear of the storm and he cast about, looking for some way to appease it. All he could think of doing was to return his daughter to her raven husband, so he grabbed Sedna and threw her overboard into the boiling, raging, icy ocean.

'But the storm did not cease, and Sedna was tossed in the stormy waves, her screams disappearing in the roar of the ocean. She was freezing now, and desperate to get back into the kayak, before she went completely numb in the frigid waters.

'She managed to swim back to the kayak and put her hand on the side of the boat, to pull herself back on board, but her father, terrified by the raging storm, thought that if he let her back into the boat she would only make the storm continue or get worse, so he grabbed the paddle and began to beat Sedna's grasping fingers. Sedna hung on desperately, screaming for her father to stop and let her into the boat, but still he hit her on the hands until at last her frozen fingers broke and fell off the side of the boat and into the water, and as they sank through the water to the bottom of the ocean, Sedna's fingers turned into seals.

'Still Sedna swam beside her father's kayak and again she reached out and clung to the side of the boat, but again her father grabbed the paddle and began beating at her hands. This time, Sedna's frozen hands broke off at her wrists and started to fall to the bottom of the sea. As they drifted down, down, down through the water, they turned into whales.

'Now Sedna had no fingers and no hands, so she couldn't find any way to get into the kayak, and her strength was sapped. She gave up the fight and began to sink.

'But she did not drown. She just spiralled down to the seabed and became the goddess of the sea. Her companions now are the seals and the whales that were created from her living fingers and hands. They live with her on the ocean bed.

'Sedna is still enraged at how her father treated her, and every now and then this fury erupts into violent storms at sea. Because of this power of hers, hunters must treat Sedna with respect, lest she unleash her anger on them and overturn their boats.

'When she is particularly angry, the shamans must swim down to the ocean bed to where Sedna sits, combing her hair that is now tangled by the sea. The shamans comb out her tangles for her and soothe her into a better mood. When she is calm, Sedna releases the sea mammals so that the people have food from the bounty of the sea. And that is why the sea yields up seals and whales and walruses in plenty for the people to eat.'

There was silence in the room when he finished.

'Well,' said Dad, after a while, 'you certainly are some storyteller, Henry.'

'Hmm,' I said. 'Cool story.'

'Yeah,' said Henry. 'Freezing story!'

We laughed but then Dad got all serious and started to explain about how stories are not just stories but are how we explain the world to ourselves.

'Dad,' I said, 'you sound like an anthropologist.'

'A what?' said Henry.

'An anthropologist,' I said, 'you know, a story stealer.'

'What?' squeaked Henry, looking all worried.

'Don't mind him, Henry,' said Dad. 'He's just teasing you. Anthropologists study stories, they don't steal them. It doesn't hurt the story. You still have the story. We can't steal it from you.'

'OK,' said Henry. 'Anyway, I just told it so Tyke would understand about the whale hunt. Sedna gives us the whales and the seals and the sea creatures for food, so it's all right if we take them for food, as long as we don't take them in anger or for money.'

It didn't make me like it any better to think of the whale being killed, but I was beginning to see what Henry meant.

17

Good News and Good News

I t was coming up to the end of July, the nalukataq was long over and the days had stretched into one endless sunny day, and Dad and I were thinking of moving on to another village for one last bit of work before the end of the summer, when there was a phone call for Dad.

Nobody ever phoned us when we were in the Arctic. When we first started going, there had been hardly any phones anyway, so we'd just got used to the idea that we didn't make contact while we were away. It was like a time out of time.

But Dad must have left Matulik's number this time, because Leah said one evening over dinner, 'Jim, you call home, you hear.'

Dad dropped his fork with a clatter.

'Call home?' he whispered. His hands were trembling.

I thought this was a bit dramatic, just because there'd been a phone call, and a strange, anticipatory feeling came over me. If people were phoning us, it must be something big. I hoped my grandad was OK. He was always having 'little turns'.

'Uh-huh,' said Leah, spooning sugar into her tea. 'Seems there's news.'

'News?' said Dad. 'What sort of news?'

'Oh,' said Leah, grinning, 'kinda surprising news, but good news and good news.'

'What? Good news and good news. What's that supposed to mean?'

'You call,' said Leah. Her English always went all foreign when she didn't want to say something.

Dad pushed his plate aside and stood up. He left the table without excusing himself, which was very unlike him, and he went out into the little lobby where Matulik's phone was.

When he came back into the room a few moments later, he was crying.

Oh my God, Grandad, I thought and rushed up to him.

'Leah said good news,' I shouted, pulling at his sleeve. 'She said *good* news!'

Dad nodded. He wiped his cheeks with the backs of his hands.

'Good news,' he managed to get out. 'And good news.'

'What is going on?' I yelled, frantic now.

Dad sat down and said in a wobbly voice: 'What do you want to hear first – the good news or the good news?'

'The good news, of course.'

'Well the good news is that you have a baby sister.'

'*What*! What! *What*!' I couldn't stop saying that one word over and over. It was such astonishing news.

At last I managed to say, 'And what's the good news?'

'Oh,' said Dad, laughing now, though there were still tears, 'the good news is that you have a baby brother.'

I put my head in my hands. I couldn't work it out. 'The good news is ... and the good news is ...'

'Oh my!' I suddenly yelped. 'Oh my! Twins!'

'Yes,' said Dad. 'Twins. One of each!'

'But I didn't even know ...'

You have to understand that it's a long time since I was a child. Kids weren't usually told when their mothers were expecting babies in those days, or not until it was almost time for the baby to be born. Of course, older children noticed, but we'd been away for so long, I hadn't had a chance to see Mum putting on weight. I couldn't imagine her pregnant. Mum with her floaty dresses and her cocktail parties. How could she go through with something so ... physical? It seemed out of character.

'How's Mum?' I asked, hardly daring to.

'She's fine. She's ecstatically happy. She sends you her love. The babies came early. Twins often do. We weren't expecting this until September. Well, we weren't expecting it to be twins at all.'

'September,' I said, remembering. 'Mum said we were to be back by September.'

'And I promised that we would. I planned to be home by mid-August in fact, but now ...'

'Dad, Mum had to go through with this on her *own*. While we were up here ... playing whalers.'

I felt really bad for Mum, and guilty about being so far away.

'Well, we didn't know, did we?' said Dad. 'But we know now, so we better get packed up and ready. We have a plane to catch, son.'

18

The Great Unicorn Hunt

The twins were lovely, of course, as babies are. Very tiny, even tinier than most babies, because of being twins and having come early. Very squirmy they were, and pink, and their shiny little mouths opened and closed a lot, as if they were trying to tell us something. Well, they were. Usually they were trying to tell us they were hungry. They were often hungry.

I was the best big brother you can imagine. I fed those kids, I changed their nappies – I did, I really did – I held one while my mum did something with the other, I bathed them, separately or together as required, I walked them up and down when they couldn't sleep and I whispered whaley stories to them as lullabies.

They got bigger, as babies do. They got to be a year old. Soon they were walking. They got to be two. Then they were talking. Not real talk, not actual words. It sounded a bit like one of Dad's arctic languages. But after a while it sort of transmogrified itself into English, beginning with the really important words, like dooce and appu and teese and toass and nana. (They had a very healthy diet in those days, before they discovered chocolate.) And, oh yes of course, Tyke.

Anyway, there was no question of Dad and me going off on expeditions to the Arctic while the babies were small. There was no way Mum could have managed them on her own. In fact, they seemed to absorb all our time as it was. It took all three of us to mind them and we seemed to do it twenty-four hours a day. Two babies seem much more than two, if you see what I mean. That is, it seems to be more than double one. Maybe it's not, but it feels that way. Maybe it's because one of them always seems to be getting into some sort of trouble when you can't get to it, because the other one has trapped you on the floor with your knees pinned behind your head and is bouncing on your face.

That's how it happened that so many years passed before Dad and I went on our next arctic trip. I never thought we'd do it again. As far as I was concerned, that was something we used to do, but early that summer when the twins were coming up to three, Dad suggested that maybe he and I might take another trip.

'I can't,' I wailed. 'Not this year. It's my Inter Cert.' That's what the Junior Cert was called when I was at school.

Dad looked blankly at me.

'Inter Cert,' he said thoughtfully, as if I'd just mentioned it to make life difficult for him. 'I suppose you have to do that.'

'Of course I have to do it. You don't want me to grow up an ignoramus, do you?'

Sometimes I got the feeling I was the grown-up and my mum and dad were the kids.

'An ignoramus. Good heavens, no,' said Dad. 'I suppose you must learn Ovid and *The Merchant of Venice* and Pythagoras' theorem and the *modh foshuíteach* and all those vitally important things.'

'Well, they *are* important,' I said.

I didn't say I'd never heard of Ovid – I didn't need to complicate the argument – but I worried that I must be an ignoramus already. They must have done it that spring term I missed when we went whaling.

'Well,' said Dad, 'we'll go after your Inter Cert. When is that?'

'June,' I said. 'I won't finish till nearly the end of June. But anyway we can't miss the twins' birthday.'

'Oh right,' said Dad, 'July that is, isn't it. Inconvenient, but …'

I glowered at him.

'We'll go in August,' he said cheerfully, as if he hadn't made that treacherous remark about July being inconvenient, 'and we'll go to Thule in Greenland. You have to see Thule, son, it's the ultimate arctic experience, the wildest place of all. We can stay till the end of September. That will suit very well. It won't hurt to miss a month of next year, will it? You haven't got any important appointments with Hamlet the Dane, have you, or Robespierre?'

I didn't like the way he said that. Snide it sounded, to me, but then it struck me that Dad really missed those trips, and taking this offhanded tone about the things that were important to me was his way of showing that. I don't think it was the anthropology he missed, either. I think it was just him and me going off together. And he chose Thule, I think, because he wanted to give me something special, 'the ultimate arctic experience' as he put it.

So I shook my head, about Robespierre I mean, and picked up a twin – we called them Tom and Tessa, by the way – and dandled it on my knee.

'The lion and the unicorn were fighting for the crown,' I told him (or her, I can't remember, though we usually colour-coded them). 'The lion beat the unicorn all about the town.'

'What about these two?' I said to Dad over the twin's shampoo-smelling curls.

'Tum dave 'em whype-bwed and tum dave 'em bwown,' said Tessa (or Tom).

'And some gave them plum cake and ran them out of town!' I finished and dropped the twin onto the carpet and ran it across the room with a whoop.

'The lion and the unicorn' was our special family nursery rhyme, because of my dad's unicorn horn, and Tom and Tessa were able to say it before they could make sentences for themselves.

'Well, your mum …'

'Dad! You always said you couldn't leave a child with Mum. You always said she'd leave it behind in a shop or something.'

'She couldn't lose two of them, though,' said Dad. 'Not even your mum could do that. And if she did, they'd look out for each other anyway.'

'Dad! They are three years old!'

'Well, I suppose we could get an *au pair*.'

'Right. An *au pair*. For two months, one of which is in the summer and one of which is in term time. Doesn't sound very likely to me.'

'We'll think of something,' said Dad, but he didn't make any more suggestions. He just sighed and gathered up his maps and charts and airline schedules and went off to his study, which he had carved out of the tiny attic, the only place, he said, in this whole damn' house where he could think.

'Wadda unicorn, Tyke?' asked one of the twins, out of the blue that evening, while we were having our dinner. Tom I think it was. He was more thoughtful than Tessa, and he took a lot of interest in the unicorn horn. We'd had to hang it high up out of his reach, but he would sit on the floor and point a small, chewed finger at it.

'A unicorn?' I said. 'You want to know what a unicorn is? Why, a unicorn is a very, very special sort of horse, Tom.'

Tom made a clopping sound with his tongue, to show that he knew what a horse was.

'That's right, a horse. A fabulous white horse. And it has a horn, see, right in the middle of its forehead.'

I picked up my knife and tipped it to the middle of my forehead, to make a horn.

The twins laughed and clapped.

'And it can fly,' I said, flapping my elbows like magic wings. I jumped up from the table and pranced about the kitchen, nodding my head to show off my horn, and scraping the floor with my hoof.

'And it flies over the ocean,' I cried, whooshing around the kitchen faster and faster, 'way, way, way over the ocean to Tír na nÓg,' I said, and I galloped and flew even faster and I made sounds like the waves as I flew.

The twins were in paroxysms of giggles by now, loving my unicorn act. They threw their little bodies about and flapped their stubby little arms, and they started to follow me around the kitchen, trying to do the unicorn actions with me.

'The unicorn loves flying over the sea,' I intoned as I flew and galloped, flew and galloped, 'because really the unicorn is a sea creature. The unicorn of the sea is its true name.'

'And guess what, twins?' Dad chipped in suddenly. 'Your big brother and I are going on a unicorn hunt!'

'What?' I said, forgetting that I was a unicorn.

'Yes,' he said. 'We're going to Thule, remember? Where the unicorn of the sea comes from.'

'Oh,' I said. I hadn't known that about Thule. 'Yes, twins, that's it. It's the Great Unicorn Hunt!'

And I pranced a bit more and shook my head and whinnied.

I meant to ask Dad what he meant about the unicorn hunt, after the twins had gone to bed, but it slipped my mind. And then I forgot all about it. I got caught up in the excitement of the trip to Thule.

19

Flying to Thule

I knew before we even went. I knew this was going to be my last trip. It wasn't exactly that I was getting too old for trips with my dad, but that I needed my summers for my own stuff. Going off like that all the time, I missed out on what was going on. Arctic trips are time-consuming. They don't really come into the same category as a weekend camping in Glendalough.

I think Dad sort of knew too. Neither of us said anything – we were being careful of each other's feelings – but there was a kind of sadness about it all, before we even started.

'We'll be fine,' Mum said, as I kissed her goodbye. 'Just come back in one piece, love.'

It hadn't occurred to me before that maybe she worried about us when we were away. She probably guessed the sorts of adventures we had, even though we didn't tell her much. She wasn't stupid, my mum. Dreamy yes, stupid no. She always looked surprised to see us when we came home from football matches, fishing trips, arctic expeditions, as if she'd forgotten these people lived here too, but sometimes

I wondered if she put on a surprised look because she didn't want to look anxious or lonely.

'You mind yourself,' I said, and gave her an extra long hug.

We had organised that my aunt and my grandad were going to take it in turns to sleep over so Mum wouldn't be on her own, and the babies were going to go to a crèche in the next street every morning, to give her a break. She'd be OK, I thought.

'This is going to be spectacular,' said Dad, as we settled into our seats on the plane. 'This is the farthest north we've ever been. It is practically the most northerly inhabited place in the world.'

The vision I'd had years before of me and Henry slumped at the foot of a North Pole that looked like a stick of rock suddenly wafted in front of my eyes. I wondered about Henry, where he was now, what he was doing, and I thought about Turaq too, and I was filled with nostalgia. I wondered if I'd make a friend this time. But perhaps I was getting too old for those intense yet casual friendships that children make.

'Spectacular' was not the sort of word my dad usually used about the north. It had that ring of tourism about it that he was so opposed to. That was the funny thing about this trip. Dad was bursting with excitement about it, but he didn't treat it like our other trips. He brought along his tape recorder, of course, but he didn't fuss about it the way he used to. It felt more like a holiday, this time, than a field trip. I think he meant it as a sort of gift to me. That touched me, but it also made me feel a little uneasy, as if I was under pressure to enjoy myself. Enjoying yourself is like sneezing.

You can't do it to order.

'I'm looking forward to it, Dad,' I said reassuringly, as I buckled my seatbelt.

'You think you've experienced the Arctic, but I tell you, you ain't seen nothing yet. You don't know cold till you've been to Thule.'

Until Dad had mentioned Thule that day back in May, I'd scarcely even heard of it, and I hadn't really thought it actually existed. I thought it was a sort of northern fairyland, like the Ice Queen's palace, not a place with an airstrip and a shop and telephone cables.

'How cold, Dad?' I asked, thinking of the levels of cold I'd experienced before on these trips with my father.

'Well, it's summer now of course,' said Dad, evasively.

'How cold?'

Dad didn't answer.

'Dad!' I said. 'Tell me.'

'Maybe six, seven degrees,' he said.

'Seven degrees! In summer! Dad – are you trying to torture me?'

'Sometimes it's warmer,' he said sheepishly.

'Oh great, so sometimes it's maybe as warm as the average winter's day in Dublin.' I said. 'Fantastic. Pity I didn't bring my swimsuit.'

'It can get up to ten or twelve degrees,' Dad said defensively.

'With lots of wind chill factor, I take it? Like I said, Dad, fantastic. I can't wait.'

'Then again, it can get *very* cold,' Dad admitted, 'even in summer. Like freezing. Or down to minus five, minus seven maybe. But you've got your snowsuit, haven't you?'

Our old joke seemed a bit washed out by now. It didn't raise a smile in me anyway.

'If it really is minus seven,' I said, 'not even a sealskin will be much good. Well, that's just great, Dad.'

But I laughed to show him I was only teasing.

20

Meeting Leon

Whenever I try to describe Thule, even to myself, it comes out like a brochure from the Greenland tourism board. You know the sort of thing: 'a crystalline landscape carved out of ice, sparkling and glistering in the high arctic summer sun'. You can't use words like that in real life to tell people what a place looks like, because they will say, 'yeah right, glistering, lovely' and will go away thinking you are daft or have overdosed on poetry or have got a job as a copywriter for a ski resort. But I promise you, this is a place that actually does glister. You have to use exotic words for Thule, because Thule itself is so outlandishly, fabulously, astoundingly exotic. In fact, there aren't words exotic enough to describe it.

'Wow!' I said when I looked out the window of the plane, as we flew north. That was as exotic as I could manage. 'Wow!'

It was like flying into an ice-cream sundae, a knickerbocker glory. The sky stretched and stretched, endlessly streaked with delicate colour, turquoise and pink, and the icy plain of snow-encased land and frozen sea stretched under it, the purest white, so white it wasn't white at all but almost blue, and here and there where crags of ice rose out of the landscape they threw pale mauve shadows on the snow. It was as if we had catapulted off the face of the earth altogether and shot away into an icing-sugar paradise, rolling and stretching and just being itself, white and glistering, over acres and acres and unimaginable acres. In fact, I wondered at first if we weren't above the cloudline; I thought maybe I was looking not at the earth at all but at the sunstreaked topsides of the clouds, the floor of heaven itself.

'Breathe out,' said my dad anxiously at my elbow.

'What?' I said, unable to take my eyes off the icy world spread out under the aeroplane.

'Whew!' said Dad. 'I thought you'd forgotten to breathe there for a minute, you were so rapt.'

He looked pleased.

'Hmm,' I said. I was breathing, but I couldn't speak. I understood now what it meant when people said something was unspeakably beautiful. When they said they couldn't find words to describe it.

'I told you it was spectacular,' Dad said smugly.

'Yes,' I said, my tongue loosened at last, 'but this … this …' And again I couldn't speak. The words just wouldn't come.

'I know what you mean,' said Dad. 'It's just … this. It's the … thisness of it, isn't it?'

'Yeah,' I said, smiling, 'that must be it, the thisness.'

It wasn't perfect, though. There were blots. The settlements, the few meagre, oily grey spots that human beings had managed to smear on this landscape, were like blemishes on the perfection of the ice. And it was into one of these human artefacts, one of these villages, that we landed.

Thule wasn't exactly camping country, unless you're a snowman, and we didn't have a contact like Matulik who might offer us a room, so we found this friendly place they called a hotel but was really more like a guest-house and that's where we stayed. We'd never stayed in a hotel before. That's part of the reason it felt more like a holiday, I suppose, this time round. And there was the language thing too. Danish is the main European language spoken in Greenland, and we didn't know much of it. People had some English, but it was broken, hesitant.

The hotel was built on blocks and the toilets were chemical. They don't have flush toilets up there, because you can't lay sewers under the ice. Nothing goes underground, not even the electricity and telephone cables – they all have to travel through the air instead of under the ground, which is part of the reason the place looks a bit ramshackle. That's also why the houses are built on blocks. You can't dig foundations, obviously, in permafrost, and you have to keep the bottom of the house out of direct contact with the ice or it might start to shift when the top layer of ice goes mulchy in the summer. And because the houses have no foundations to keep them steady, they have to weigh them down with great walloping metal drums full of bricks so they don't blow away in the arctic wind. But we had comfortable beds and they gave us food when we asked for it. Dad was in heaven.

We hung about the village for a bit, trying to find people to talk to, but the ice-breaker had just opened up the harbour, and ships were berthing day after day, and everyone who was able to work was down at the docks unloading supplies. The harbour only stays open for a few weeks, and then it starts to freeze over again for the winter, so everything the villagers are going to need for the whole year has to be landed in these few weeks. And the people that weren't busy at the harbour seemed to be building. They have a joke up there that there are four seasons: nearly winter, winter, still winter and construction. I'd heard that joke about the Arctic before, only with mosquitoes instead of construction. But that was one thing about Thule – too cold even for arctic mosquitoes.

'Patience,' Dad said. 'We'll just have to wait for a bit.'

I didn't know what he meant. I wasn't feeling impatient, or at least I didn't think I was. I wasn't expecting anything in particular.

One evening, we met an oldish man at the hotel, a shrunken, weather-beaten sort of a person with a scar across his face and running down into his neck. He came in for a cup of tea and to watch the news on the TV. Dad got talking to him. His name was Leon and he told us he was a hunter. Dad started to squirm with excitement. He nodded to me, as it to say, Here it comes, now, didn't I tell you!

Leon liked to live the old way of life, he said, and to catch what he could to make a living. He didn't hold with all the developments in the area, distracting the men from the real work of the Greenlander, which is fishing and hunting and finding food. And selling the other produce of the animals, like oil or pelts.

'I see they get job,' he said. 'That good, they got money

in they pocket. But they trap'. They can' go hunting when weather right. They can only hunt weekends. So they take a time off to hunt, then the boss, he get mad, he say Inuk worker lazy, no good.'

He was just like any old man you meet anywhere, shaking his grey old head and giving out about change, but Dad found his views very interesting. He sat up late that night writing things in his notebook.

Leon complained a bit more about development and about how the price of sealskins had slumped on the world market because of pressure from animal lovers. He complained about how you couldn't export ivory products either. I thought he was thinking on a global scale, comparing the sealskin problem here with the ivory harvest in India or Africa or somewhere like that. I really didn't want to get into the ivory debate, so I sat still and said nothing, but I was churning up a bit inside. It reminded me of how uneasy I had felt about the bowhead hunt. I thought I'd resolved my feelings about that, but evidently I hadn't, not completely.

Leon was going hunting the next day, he said, him and his team of dogs. I could see that Dad was practically expiring with the desire to ask him if we could go along, but he wasn't sure if the old man would think that impolite. Dad always said that other peoples had different standards for what was polite, and so you never just went by your own feeling for it. You had to watch the behaviour of people around you to find out what was acceptable.

But I didn't have my dad's finely tuned anthropologist's sensibilities, and I thought I could probably get away with being more forthright, since I was young. So I just came straight out and asked.

'You have a team of dogs, Leon? Gosh! And you're going hunting tomorrow. Could you take a couple of passengers, do you think?'

Dad looked at the ceiling, looked at the floor, looked anywhere but at Leon in case he had the wrong expression on his face.

Leon nodded. 'Sure,' he said.

Dad beamed.

'I drive tourists, often,' Leon went on complacently.

Dad's face fell. Tourists! He opened his mouth, I am sure, to explain to Leon that we weren't tourists, but then he must have thought better of it, because he closed his mouth again. Then he opened it for a second time and said, 'Well, that's settled then. *Mange tak*, Leon. Will we see you here at the hotel then, tomorrow?'

'Sure,' said Leon again.

'Now you'll see,' said Dad later. 'At least, I think you will.'

'What?' I asked.

'What I promised,' said Dad.

I didn't know what he was talking about. I'd forgotten all about the unicorn hunt, and if he'd mentioned it, I'd have thought he was romancing.

Hunting the Narwhal

We waited for Leon the next day, but he never arrived. Dad was disappointed, but he put a brave face on it. He said maybe it had something to do with the weather conditions, and that Leon would probably come the following day. But he didn't. Nor the next day. By the end of a week, I'd given up on old Leon. Dad was tense – I could see he thought the whole expedition had been a bit of a failure – and in the end, he gave up on him too.

'We'll go soon,' he said, noticing my restlessness. 'Next week. Or maybe the week after.' He sounded sort of wistful, like a child trying to negotiate a later bedtime, but not expecting to have much luck.

I didn't say anything. It really was time to be thinking about getting home. The nights were drawing in, and the temperature was already starting to drop sharply at sunset. I had to get back to school, and besides, I missed Mum and the twins.

'Leon leave a message for you, Mr Jim,' Bebe said one morning, about the time we were thinking of leaving. Bebe was the woman who ran our hotel. It tickled Dad no end the way she called him 'Mr Jim'.

'Leon?' Dad's eyes lit up. 'What did he say?'

'He say to tell you, they all goin' to the narwhal hunt over to the fjord. He thought you might like to go watch.'

Dad's excitement was obvious. He instantly forgave Leon for not having appeared to take us hunting.

'This is it, son! The narwhal hunt!'

'Narwhal?' I said. 'What's a narwhal, Dad?'

'You don't know what a *narwhal* is?' Dad looked shocked, as if I'd said I didn't know that Paris was the capital of France or my five times tables.

'Should I?'

'The narwhal,' said Dad, standing up from the breakfast table and pushing his chair in with a grand gesture of impatience, 'is the u....' Suddenly he dropped his grand tone, as if he thought I might think he was being silly. 'Well, actually,' he said, in a more ordinary tone of voice, 'it's a rather small whale. Unusual though, very unusual. Just wait and see.'

He was making it all very mysterious. I shrugged, but for some unnamed reason, an image of myself in a velvet cloak, lined with stars, floated through my mind.

'Did he say he would come for us?' Dad asked Bebe. 'Leon, I mean.'

She shook her head. Dad's face fell.

'You want I ask my sister's boy to take you over there?' Bebe asked. 'Leon say Michael can take you if you like.'

Dad practically whimpered with excitement. 'Please,' he said, 'oh please do. And you,' he said to me, 'do I take it that you want to come?'

Poor Dad. He knew I wasn't very keen on whale-hunting. But he desperately wanted me to come – and to want to come. He was right. I didn't like it, but after the bowhead hunt, I'd come to some sort of an arrangement in my head about it, an agreement with myself to tolerate it. I decided I'd go with him, this one last time, and I wouldn't argue about it.

When Bebe's nephew arrived, he had polar-bearskin trousers for us to wear. I looked at the shaggy things, and I looked at Dad, and I said: 'Do I have to?'

'You will be so glad of these trousers, you know. Polar-bearskin is the warmest fur in the world.'

Michael nodded. 'Keep out the cold, keep out the wind, keep out the water.' He was about my age, I think, but he had a wise air about him, like an old man.

'But it looks like I'm wearing a sheepskin rug. I look like a caveman.'

'It doesn't matter what you look like,' Dad said, 'but what you actually look like is a Kalaallit hunter.'

So we bundled up in all the skins and furs Michael had brought us, and we waddled, like two walking haystacks, down the hotel steps. Tied up at the porch was a sled with a team of ten creamy white and dashingly handsome huskies. They looked all freshly brushed and as soon as they saw us emerging, they set up a whine of welcome. I went to pat their heads, but Michael shouted at me.

'Don't! These dogs aren't pets. They wolves.'

'Oh!' I said, and pulled my hand back.

'These are Leon's dogs,' he went on. 'They good dogs, well trained, but they can turn nasty.'

'Nasty?'

'Yup. Leon attacked by a husky once out on the ice. The food ran out. The dog went mad with hunger. Leon still got the scar.'

'Ouch!' I said. 'But how come you don't use snowmobiles or scooters?'

'Ach,' said Michael, 'snowmobiles break down. Your snowmobile breaks down, you're out on the ice, what you do? Walk home? Dogs don't break down.'

'That's right,' said Dad, looking pleased as punch. 'Dogs don't break down.'

They just go mad and attack you, I thought, but I didn't say so. I just kept a wary eye on the dogs as I climbed onto the sled.

Suddenly, almost before we had settled, Michael had whisked up the dogs' attention with a shouted command, and we were off, skimming over the ice, like the Snow Queen, watching the cloudy mists of the dogs' breath rising up in the still air before us.

The dogs raced and raced, scooping up snow to drink as they ran, without pausing. Pretty soon, we had left the village miles behind, and still we skimmed over the ice, for miles and miles into the icy wilderness. Our faces froze, but our bodies were warm under our skins and furs, and even our feet felt pinky-warm in their layers of socks.

There seemed to be more of this landscape than you could possibly imagine. It stretched out for ever. The sky, dove grey with clouds today, was low over the ice. You felt you could almost reach out and touch it, and that it would be soft and warm, though of course, even if you could reach it, it would be cold and misty.

After what seemed like hours, Michael called something to the huskies and they stopped, quite suddenly. While the dogs lay panting on the snow, Michael untangled the seal-skin lines that tied them to the sled. The dogs didn't take any notice. They lay quietly, huddled into groups for warmth.

'Need to rest the dogs,' Michael said, by way of explanation, and then he started to make conversation. 'You go to school?'

'Yes.' I said. 'Two more years. Then college.'

It felt a bit weird to be discussing my education out here in the middle of the icy landscape, but of course to Michael, this was all perfectly normal.

'You want to be a doctor,' he said.

It wasn't a question. He said it as if it was a fact, the only possible reason for wanting to go to college.

'Not a doctor,' I said.

'You want to be a *teacher*?' he said incredulously.

'No,' I said, 'not a teacher.'

Funny that I ended up teaching after all, though what I meant was that I didn't want to teach in a school. University's different.

'Well, what then?' asked Michael.

'A … a …' I began, hoping something would occur to me. 'I don't know,' I concluded lamely.

'You want to go to college, you don't know what you want to be.' Michael clearly thought I was a bit of a twit.

'I want to study,' I said defensively.

'What you want to study?'

'History,' I said.

I was surprised to hear myself say it, but I was even more

surprised to discover I meant it. I didn't know what you could *be* if you studied history, but I knew I wanted to do it anyway.

'Wars,' he said dismissively. 'History all wars.'

'No,' I said, 'history's all stories.'

'You don't want to be an anthropologist?' Dad said in a mock-disappointed tone.

I knew I was supposed to step back in horror at the idea and say under no circumstances or something exaggerated, but I didn't feel like playing that game.

'Not an anthropologist,' I said, 'but it's close, isn't it, Dad?'

'Oh, that's too profound for me,' Dad said, but he looked pretty pleased all the same.

'What do you want to be, Michael?' I asked. 'A hunter?'

I don't know why I assumed that. No reason why he couldn't be whatever he liked.

'No. I want a job. I want money. I want to move to some-place where things happen.'

I laughed at the idea that nothing happened here, but it was a hollow laugh. I knew exactly what he meant. Maybe it had something to do with being fifteen.

The dogs must have been rested by then, because Michael picked up the reins and we were off again.

I poked Dad in the side as we sped along.

'What?' he asked.

'Just hello,' I said.

'Just hello yourself,' he said and smiled at me.

'That sky looks like snow,' Dad called to Michael.

Michael shook his head. 'Naw,' he said, 'snow unusual here.'

I looked around incredulously at the vast snowy land-scape and I laughed.

'Right,' I said. 'I can see that.'

'Oh, this take years. It don't snow much, but it build up.'

'It certainly does,' I said.

When we arrived at the fjord, Michael stopped the sled at a good distance from the water, so as not to disturb the hunt, and we left the dogs huddled up together for another rest. We crouched in the cover of a huge lump of ice like a small cliff to watch the hunters from a distance.

The kayaks were already out on the water. It was completely different from the bowhead hunt we'd seen all those years ago, no whaling crews, just individual hunters in their individual little boats. The hunters sat still, waiting for a sighting of a narwhal. The trick was to keep very quiet so as to be able to surprise the creature. If the narwhal had any warning, it would probably escape and that would be the end of hunting for all the hunters for that day.

We spotted Leon on the water. He sat hunched with his face peering out of his parka like an old walnut, not making a sound, not a ripple on the water. He didn't look like a tourist guide today. He looked like a man with a job to do.

We watched and waited, and watched and waited for what seemed like hours, our limbs stiffening and freezing as we crouched uncomfortably.

Then, entirely without warning, in a single movement, Leon threw his harpoon. It sliced the air and hit its target almost at the same time. I tensed for the explosion, but it didn't happen. Instead, Leon made a swift movement with his lance. I couldn't see the narwhal, as it was shielded from my view by Leon's body, but I knew by the way he wielded the lance and the way the movement stopped so swiftly that he had killed it with a single stabbing motion. I was glad about that. I couldn't have borne it if the creature had bellowed in pain and thrashed the water and had a long, slow death.

When the younger men had helped Leon to manoeuvre the narwhal to shore, I managed to get glimpses of it between the moving bodies on the shoreline. It was the strangest-looking creature. It looked like a very large, bloated dolphin, streaked with its own blood, awkward and sodden in death, not magnificent at all, as the bowhead had been. The oddest thing was that, as far as I could see from where we stood – our view was intermittent, constantly being blocked by the movements of the hunters – Leon's spear seemed to be stuck right through the head of the narwhal, so that it looked as if it had grown an unwieldy tusk, as long as its own body, or longer. It looked a bit like an overweight swordfish.

'The meat has to be shared,' Michael explained, 'but the hunter who kill the narwhal, he get the tusk.'

'Oh, so it is a tusk then,' I said.

'Of course it's a tusk,' said Dad. 'It's a narwhal. Surely you know now what I mean about the narwhal being an unusual whale? I mean it's the tusked whale.'

'Dad, I don't know what you're talking about,' I said, as we watched while Leon cut the tusk from the narwhal's forehead. 'You talk as if I should know everything there is to know about narwhals, but I've never even heard the word before today.'

'But the tusk,' said Dad. 'The tusk. We've had that tusk for ever. You must remember the tusk.'

'What tusk?' I asked.

'In the sitting room at home,' Dad said. 'The one you used to pretend was a unicorn horn when you were small. The one you told Tom and Tessa about before we came away, remember, when you were being a unicorn?'

'What do you mean, I used to *pretend* it was a unicorn horn? It *is* a unicorn horn. You always said it was.'

'Taig,' said Dad, 'you are fifteen years old. You know the dreadful truth about Santa Claus. Surely you don't think that the narwhal tusk we have at home is a unicorn horn!'

'But of course I do!' I exclaimed. 'Did, I mean, until this minute. You *said* so Dad, you always said so.'

I could feel hot, shameful tears gathering behind my eyes as I realised my error. All those years, I'd believed in unicorns, and I'd believed it, not out of some childish naïveté, but because I had scientific proof on the wall of my own sitting room at home. I'd never questioned it, never had a reason to question it.

But now, here in front of me was Leon brandishing a narwhal tusk that he had just hacked off a fat, stubby, dead and undignified whale. The tusk oozed blood. It looked nothing like a unicorn horn. It looked like a big, ugly, gnarled, overgrown tooth with the bloody roots attached. It did spiral, like a unicorn horn, but there was certainly no seam of gold running up through it. This great clump of a thing had never graced the head of a fabulous white horse that flew over the sea. As I watched Leon hacking at the roots of the narwhal tusk with his knife to free it of blood and meat, I could see with another eye my star-lined velvet cloak floating off over the sea and disappearing beyond the horizon.

It looked from this angle, the way he stood over the small

whale's body, almost as if Leon was tussling with the narwhal for the tusk. Leon, I thought, Leon means lion.

'Look,' I said. 'The lion and the unicorn are fighting for the crown. The unicorn of the sea, Dad. You always said the horn belonged to the unicorn of the sea.'

'Yes,' said Dad. 'That's what the narwhal is called. It's a sort of pet name or nickname. The unicorn of the sea.'

'So there are no unicorns,' I whispered.

'Son, there are no unicorns.'

'You told Tessa and Tom we were going on a unicorn hunt,' I said accusingly.

'Yes, I did. But Tessa and Tom are three years old. That's the sort of story you tell babies. You pretended you could fly! But you can't fly, and there are no unicorns.'

But then, there are narwhals. When you think about it, that's pretty amazing in itself. What on earth does a whale need with a great long tusk like that? It's too fragile to be any good as a yoke for poking around looking for food, and it's too awkward to do anything else with. The narwhal is a fantastic enough sort of a creature if fantastic is what you are after. But at the time, it didn't seem much of a compensation. I didn't see myself riding a narwhal wearing a cloak spangled with stars. It just wasn't the same.

Whistling to the Aurora

Two days later, we flew to Copenhagen in broad arctic
daylight, and we arrived in ordinary European night. We
had several hours before we could catch our connection to
Heathrow and on to Dublin. As the night thickened, the
airport went into that curious lulled state you get at night
in places that never sleep, like airports and hospitals. The
lights are on, but they're slightly dimmed, in deference to
the patients or passengers who are trying to snatch a bit of
shuteye, and the non-essential services, like the cafeteria,
shut down for a few hours. In that hour before the early
shift arrives with mops, and the hiss of the coffee-machine
starts up again, the poor demented souls who are waiting
endlessly in the wide, tiled, echoing corridors or foyers go
into a trance that is not quite sleep and not quite the waking state either, a sort of suspended animation, where the
nerves are somehow more alert than normal and ready to
spring into panic, even though the other organs of the body
seem to slow down as in sleep.

This was the state I was in at about four in the morning,

with my rucksack on my knee, when Dad suddenly nudged me and started calling my name in a loud, urgent whisper.

'Wake up, wake up! Oh, you'll never guess, it is so fabulous! Wake up, can't you!'

I opened my eyes, exposing my eyeballs to the assault of the waking world. Dad was hopping on the spot in front of me, and pointing out the wide, wide glass barrier that served as both wall and window, into the night sky. At the very least, it had to be a unicorn flying across the stars, I thought, to make him so excited.

'Damn these planes,' he muttered. It would have been funny if I'd been wider awake, Dad swearing about planes at an airport. 'They keep interfering. They come in to land and everywhere lights up like a Christmas tree. Oh, there it is again, now, quick, now, before another wretched plane comes, quick, quick, while it's dark. Just our luck to be at an airport at a time like this.'

'What am I looking for?' I asked, my head feeling like a leaden ball on my neck.

'The lights, the lights!' Dad practically shouted.

I looked up at the dimmed overhead lights.

'No, no, the Aurora, the Aurora Borealis, look, look, look, it's the Northern Lights. I've never seen them so far south before. Isn't it wonderful?'

I screwed up my eyes and looked where his frantic finger was pointing, and sure enough, across the navy tent of the clear night sky outside the enormous expanse of airport glass, I saw a streak of red and a streak of green, followed by a streak of red and a streak of green, as if someone was pulling a huge, airy red and green curtain across the stars.

135

'Wow!' said Dad. 'Oh wow!'

I could hear tears in his voice. I looked at him, and his eyes were glistening.

'Just imagine what this looks like in Thule,' he said.

Thule spread in front of my mind again, the starry autumn night doming the moongleamed icy floor. And as I watched the Northern Lights flit softly over the Copenhagen sky, I could see them also in my mind's eye wafting eerily across the icy landscape we had just left.

'A shame we didn't see it in Thule,' I said. 'Would we have seen it if we'd stayed a bit longer, if we were there tonight?' I added guiltily.

'No, probably not. It's almost too far north to get a good view in Thule,' Dad said. 'They rarely appear there.'

Just then we heard a whistling sound, eerie and sudden. It was repeated and repeated, high-pitched and urgent. It seemed to be coming from near by, inside the airport building. I turned my head, to see who it was that was whistling. Everyone was half-asleep, half-aroused by the whistling. Everyone except the squat orange-clad figure of an early-morning cleaner wielding a huge industrial floor-cleaning machine. The cleaner stood like us at the sheet of window and stared out into the night sky, his cleaning machine abandoned, his hands pressed flat against the glass. He whistled again, and then he turned a cheerful face to us. A cheerful Inuit face.

Dad said: 'Must be a Greenlander. Lots of Greenlanders work in Copenhagen.'

He waved over at the cleaner. 'Whistling at the Aurora?' he called.

The man grinned and made a thumbs-up gesture, to show

he understood. He nodded and smiled and waved his thumb a bit more, jerking it in the direction of the lights outside the window, and then he turned and started pushing his cleaning machine. He was pushing it in our direction.

'The children of the Arctic whistle when they see the Aurora Borealis,' Dad said. 'They believe if they whistle, they can make the lights come down to earth, they can prolong the lights. They only appear at night, of course, and when you think what night means up there in the high north, anything that lights the night is well worth cultivating.'

By now the cleaner had reached us, and we could see that he was quite old.

'Whistle,' he said.

We smiled at him.

'In the Arctic,' Dad said to me, 'the people believe that the Northern Lights are torches that the spirits of the dead light to guide the souls of people who have just died up into heaven. Isn't that right?' he added, to the cleaner.

The old man nodded. 'Stars,' he said, pointing out at the sky.

'Yes,' said Dad. 'The souls can get into heaven through little holes in the dome of the sky. The little holes are the stars, where the light shines through from heaven.'

'Stars,' said the cleaner again. 'Lights. Whistle.'

'I think he wants us to whistle, Dad,' I said. 'Let's whistle to the Aurora.'

'Don't be daft,' Dad said, looking around at the other passengers slumped in the airport chairs, their chins on their chests.

But I whistled anyway, softly, so as not to wake the

137

snoozing people. My cleaner friend whistled too.

'I have to be able to tell Tessa and Tom I whistled,' I explained.

'Tessa and Tom,' said Dad, vaguely, as if he'd only just remembered he had other children.

Then he said: 'How long do you think before they'll be ready to come to the Arctic, Tyke?'

He'd never called me by my arctic nickname before. I knew then what I'd only vaguely thought before. I knew then for sure that he knew that this was my last trip.

'Oh, pretty soon, Dad,' I said. 'Pretty soon. And twins will go down a treat, don't you think?'

'I think,' Dad said, and he laughed.

The cleaner laughed too, and trundled on by with his machine.

Epilogue

Tessa and Tom are grown up now too, of course. Tessa works in television, making wildlife programmes, and Tom is a veterinarian, specialising in sea mammals. As you can guess, they both took many trips to the Arctic with Dad when they were children, mainly in the summer time, which is probably why neither of them has ever seen the Aurora Borealis.

I really do mean to keep in touch with Henry this time. Meeting him in Geneva spread my whole arctic past in front of me again, a past I don't often revisit, but a past I couldn't shake off even if I wanted to. Things have changed beyond recognition now in the Arctic, except maybe in Thule, and I was privileged, as a boy – though I didn't know it at the time – to get even glimpses of a way of life that is now only preserved in small remote pockets and by the efforts of people like my friend Henry.

They say you shouldn't go back, you should never try to revisit your childhood, but I think I will. I can't resist it. I've tried, but I can't. I can't resist it because the song of the whale is like a call to the north. I hear it in my sleep. Eerie and sonorous, it pervades my dreams, so that I am drawn down into the deep, where huge sea beasts roll slowly in the inky-cold seas, wailing for their lovers over acres of waters.

I wake, gasping for air, from these whaley dreams, but even though I wake, I cannot seem to shake off the dream. All day the whales are with me, as I work my way through my city schedule – breakfast, train, work, lunch, work, drink, train, dinner, TV, bed – swishing their powerful tails, diving uproariously to the seabed, drifting in the depths and then slowly, slowly, like the air leaking out of a tyre, ballooning up and up and up to crash onto the surface once again and exhale their fabulous fountainy breath …

Also by SIOBHÁN PARKINSON

FOUR KIDS, THREE CATS, TWO COWS, ONE WITCH (maybe)

Beverly, a bit of a snob, cooks up a plot to visit the island off the coast. She manages to convince the somewhat cautious Elizabeth and her slob of a brother, Gerard, to go with her. Then there's a surprise companion – Kevin, the cool guy who works in the local shop. This motley crew must find ways to support each other, and put up with one another's shortcomings, when they become stranded on the island and encounter a strange inhabitant.

Paperback £4.99/€6.34/$7.95

THE MOON KING

Ricky has withdrawn from the world into his own inner space. Placed in a foster home that is full of sunshine and goodness, he is uncertain how to become part of family life. He often retreats to his favourite hideaway – a special chair in the attic, and adopts the pose of the Moon King. Slowly, relationships begin to grow, but it is not a smooth path and at times Ricky just wants to leave it all behind.

Paperback £4.99/€6.34/$7.95

SISTERS ... NO WAY!

Cindy, a with-it and cynical young teen, still traumatised by her mother's recent death, is appalled when her father falls in love with one of her teachers, a woman with two prissy teenage daughters. Surely he can't be serious? She cannot imagine a worse fate than having a teacher as her stepmother, and as for the two girls – she is never going to call them sisters ... no way! But if Cindy dislikes her prospective stepsisters, they think she is an absolute horror – spoiled, arrogant and atrociously rude. They can't imagine being landed with Cindy as a sister ... no way! An amusing and touching story about change and growing up.

Paperback £4.99/€6.34/$7.95

AMELIA

The year is 1914 and Amelia Pim will soon be thirteen. There are rumours of war and rebellion, and Dublin is holding its breath for a major upheaval. But all that matters to Amelia is what she will wear to her birthday party. Then disaster strikes the Pim family? When Mama's political activities bring the final disgrace, it is Amelia who must hold the family together. Only the friendship of the servant girl Mary Ann seems to promise any hope.

Paperback £4.99/€6.34/$7.95

NO PEACE FOR AMELIA

It's 1916, but Amelia Pim's thoughts are on Frederick Goodbody and not on the war in Europe. Then Frederick enlists. The pacifist Quaker community is shocked, but Amelia is secretly proud of her hero and goes to the quayside to wave him farewell. For her friend Mary Ann, there are problems too, with her brother's involvement in the Easter Rising. What will become of the two young men and what effect will it have on the lives of Amelia and Mary Ann?

Paperback £4.99/€6.34/$7.95

Send for our full-colour catalogue